The Initiation

No one sleeps much before his first combat. . . .
People start getting up hours before they have to.
You take extra care shaving and dressing.

Steak and eggs is the traditional Marine breakfast before a landing. No one feels much like eating
now. Your mouth is dry, and the food tastes like
cotton. . . .

In the helicopter you keep thinking what it would
be like to get shot. You have never seen combat
before and you wonder if it is really like all those
briefings you got back in the States and on Okinawa.
You remember the officers and men who briefed
you on their experiences in Vietnam. They seemed
strange — distant. You wonder if you'll become like
them.

point

YOUNG MAN IN VIETNAM

Charles Coe

SCHOLASTIC INC.
New York Toronto London Auckland Sydney

ISBN 0-590-43298-2

12 11 10 9 8 7 6 5 4 3 2 1   0 1 2 3 4 5/9

Printed in the U.S.A.   01

First Scholastic printing, January 1990

Contents

Preface
to the
Paperback Edition

Dear Tommy and Charlie:

More than twenty years have passed since I wrote *Young Man in Vietnam*. The world has turned over many times since then; a whole generation of things has happened to me — jobs, marriage, divorce, loves, deaths. And most special of all, you two fine sons arrived.

Vietnam has faded from the news. No more daily television reports. No more frenzied protests in the streets. No more telegrams announcing casualties. The war, it seems, belongs now to history.

Historians will write about it as they always do in terms of the winners . . . the losers . . . of the political ramifications. Somehow in the process, what it meant for those of us who were there is lost.

I wrote this book twenty years ago because I felt then what happened on a daily basis was important to record. Not the "big" things historians write about. The things that truly mattered to those of us who fought. A letter from home. Your first dead man. The heat. The boredom. The fear.

I'm glad I had the experience of being a young man in Vietnam. I wouldn't trade it for anything. But I could never go through it again. At least not in the same way. The experience never leaves you where it finds you.

I hope this book rings true to you. I hope it has more meaning than just the fact your father wrote it. I hope it will tell you something about me long after I am gone. I hope it tells you that, as horrible as war is, it is possible to fight one without losing your soul or your sense of honor or your profound awe at human strength. But most of all, I hope you never have to fight a war.

Your loving father.

Charles Coe
May 15, 1989

YOUNG MAN IN VIETNAM

Das Schwert ist kein Spaten, kein Pflug,
Wer damit ackern wollte, wäre nicht klug.

The sword is no spade, no plow, and to use it
To dig in the fields would be to abuse it.

                  Schiller (*Wallenstein's Lager*)

1
The Beginning

The ground is still wet from the night's rain and everything smells clean and fresh. The sun is beginning to burn off the ground fog and it feels warm on your face when you look up. You watch the patrol sliding down the hillside toward your hidden position. There are twelve men in the patrol. They are bunched up and moving quickly. They want to get home.

You look at your machine gunners and they smile.

"This one's going to be too easy, Lieutenant," one of them whispers.

You nod for him to be quiet. Wires stretch from the detonator at your feet through the underbrush to a series of explosive charges placed near the trail the patrol must move down.

As you wait for the patrol, you reach down and touch the handle of the detonator. It is very smooth and wet and you hope the dampness hasn't affected the charges. When the third man in the patrol has passed your position, you press the handle and the explosive roars its greeting.

Your machine gunners open fire at once. They are firing as fast as they can from three different positions and the staccato of the individual guns blends into a uniform hammering. The patrol leader shouts and tries to rally his men, but they are hopelessly confused. They aren't even returning the fire.

"Cease fire," you yell. "Cease fire."

The sudden silence is shattering. You order the patrol leader to assemble his men at a large oak tree about a hundred meters distant for a critique of the exercise.

As you walk to the tree you think of the other patrols that have been run since you took command of the NCO Leadership School. You check your notebook for some of the specific mistakes this patrol committed. It will be a long critique.

You enter your office after dismissing the patrol for the morning and your admin chief hands you a note. He says it's important. The note is from Jan, a friend in your old infantry battalion. He's the intelligence officer there. The note asks you to call him right away.

"Welcome aboard," he says.

"What do you mean?"

"You will shortly."

"Listen, should I dig out Esther's address? I've got it here someplace." You are kidding him about a girl he knew in the Philippines when you were overseas together a year earlier. And you are asking him to confirm what you have both known by rumor for at least a week — the battalion is going back overseas.

"You'd better find Big Ida's, too," he says.

You tell him you'll meet him for lunch in a few minutes and you feel your stomach tightening with excitement.

You hardly recognize the battalion area. There are crates of gear stacked everywhere. No one is drilling troops or holding inspections or teaching classes. There is barbed wire strung around the CP, and armed guards are patrolling. You ask the sentry at the entrance to the CP if your friend is there and he checks a list for your name before he tells you to go in.

"For Christ's sake, what's going on?" you greet Jan.

"You're looking at it. We're going back and you're going with us."

"Don't I have any choice?" you protest.

"The orders are already cut. They knew you'd volunteer. Besides, if you tell them no you'll make paperwork for a dozen clerks and two dozen majors. And you know what that would mean." He takes a pencil out of his pocket and begins to initial reports that are stacked on his desk. "Look," he says, "everybody is going to be back in Asia before too very long. At least you can go back with some people you know — your old battalion."

"That's what I'm afraid of," you tell him. You knew from the minute you talked with him on the phone that you would go — that you wanted to. You

5

dislike being told you have to do anything, but you know you'll go. "I guess I'd better find those addresses," you grin at him.

"*Semper Fi*," he says.

You receive orders as soon as you are back at your office. The Director of the Schools Battalion calls you in and asks if you want to return to the Second Battalion the next day. He wishes you luck and you shake hands with him and leave quickly.

Your company commander is new to the infantry. He has come from duty with a guard detachment at a naval station. He relies on you as the executive officer — and the second in command — to get things done. You like the responsibility.

They are bringing the battalion up to full strength and many new people are posted to your company. There are assignments to be made and briefings to be attended. You know you'll be leaving the States soon — maybe within the week, but the exact date hasn't been released yet.

You make sure your men have all their field gear. You have the company armorer check all the weapons and you replace those that fail the examination. The corpsmen are busy giving shots — typhus, cholera, typhoid, plague. There are division orders to be reviewed and regimental directives to be filed and battalion reports to be completed. By the end of the week you are exhausted. You are having a hard time keeping your sense of humor. But when you think of what you'll soon be doing the excitement makes a sense of humor seem unimportant.

Word comes down on Friday that you'll be leaving the next day. The electric effect you thought it would have isn't there. Everyone is too weary; everything is too confused. You caution your men not to reveal the sailing time and you let them go on their last liberty in the United States.

You drive up to Laguna Beach with Jack. You go to a little bar and drink beer until you're very drunk. The beer is free. Tommy, the bartender, says he wishes he were going with you. Everyone is slapping you on the back and wishing you luck and shaking your hand. Through the beer haze you enjoy the recognition and you try not to brag. But you're proud to be a Marine and you're happy — even anxious — to be going into combat. You'll prove to yourself at last what the training has told you — that you're the best.

By dusk you are ready to drive back to Camp Pendleton. You can see the ocean swelling and flexing in the fading twilight and the smell of it is very strong. You pass your old home in San Clemente and you feel a twinge of homesickness. You won't be sleeping there anymore.

There are buses waiting to take the outfit to your ship in San Diego. Everyone has been drinking and it is hard to load the vehicles. People are sleeping on their packs all around the parade deck and someone is constantly getting sick. The officers and staff are checking rosters and yelling and looking for stray Marines. By midnight the buses are loaded and rolling to San Diego. No one in your company is AWOL.

You try to sleep on the bus. The beer is beginning

to wear off and the seat is too small for you and your pack. The lights of oncoming vehicles make you blink. You feel sick to your stomach. You drank too much. But it won't be long now.

The ship looms up at dockside like a skyscraper. You think it is part of the pier — that even if you chopped all the lines securing it, it couldn't float away.

Your company boards last. You take off your pack and sit on it by the gangway and watch the other companies file onto the ship. There is a constant stream of olive drab figures. You think it will never end.

When your company is called away, you and your first sergeant check the name of each Marine against a master roster as he moves up the gangway. You make sure all your men have bunks and that their gear is properly stored before you move to the Troop Officers' Quarters to find your berth.

It is just sunrise. You feel the ship throb gently and the announcement comes over the intercom that you are underway. Some of the officers are going out to the weather decks to watch America slide away in the distance. But you are too tired. You aren't interested in what is behind. You know you'll see the States again. It's only a year.

2
The Trip

You're two days out of San Diego on the USS *Bexar* and rain sweeps in sheets across the ship. There is green water breaking over the bow and the Navy has rigged ropes on the weather decks. You can steady yourself on the ropes when you have to move. There are two weeks to go.

Most of the troops are billeted in the forward berthing compartments. During rough weather they aren't permitted on the open decks. But most of them are too sick to go topside. There isn't much you can say to someone who is seasick. You leave him alone.

You have administrative duties and rough weather is a good time to accomplish them. At least you know where everyone is — in his rack. Service record books are checked and emergency data is verified. Lists are made of next of kin, and the battalion legal officer mimeographs wills for you to distribute to the troops. When you file your final embarkation report you have nothing left to do — but wait.

The ship is too crowded to permit any training. Most of the time is spent reading or writing letters or watching the sea roll by. The men have to stand in the chow line about two hours for each meal. They sleep the rest of their free time — curled around winches, under exhaust screens, against bulkheads, beside ladder wells, anywhere there is unoccupied space.

You are a week out and a rumor has started. You hear it first in the wardroom and later in the afternoon your supply sergeant mentions it. Golf clubs. Someone has brought their golf clubs aboard and the battalion executive officer wants to know who. You don't go to war with golf clubs.

The next morning the executive officer assembles the company supply sergeants. Armed with wirecutters and crowbars they investigate all boxed gear stored topside. The gear is packed in watertight crates and sealed and banded so the salt air and water won't damage equipment. You have no facilities to reseal the boxes.

You know where the golf clubs are. You helped pack them. And you make it a point to be there when your company's crates are searched. By this time the decks are awash with banding cables and weather stripping and broken boards. Metal gear already blushes with the first tinges of rust. Supply sergeants are cursing and trying to stuff their newly liberated equipment back into boxes. Your company is inspected last.

The golf clubs are wrapped in brown paper and you're afraid the executive officer will miss them. When the box is opened you reach down and pull out a mashie far enough for him to see. He bellows in triumph and rips out great handfuls of paper and tosses them skyward. As he continues to shred the paper a name begins to appear on the bag. When the stenciled name and rank of the battalion commander becomes visible, the executive officer stops tearing paper. A strange, faraway look comes into his eyes and he turns very slowly toward the bridge and walks away — sliding his hand loosely along the railing. You tell your supply sergeant to stop grinning and begin repacking the gear.

Five of you had been overseas together last year. You have smuggled some whiskey aboard and you decide to celebrate your return to Asia.

One of the naval officers will let you use his stateroom — for a bottle. You consider — half-seriously — throwing him overboard one dark night and celebrating that by using his quarters. But you finally agree on a pint for him and a few free hours in his room for you.

Liquor is strictly forbidden on American warships — except for medicinal purposes. Its possession is a general court-martial offense. But when you're going into combat in a few weeks no one bothers about court-martials.

You have a fifth of bourbon and the whiskey

burns your throat as you drink it. But it tastes good. There is no formality here. You just pass the bottle around. You're all excited about the prospect of combat. Your old battalion participated in some relief work at Da Nang and Qui Nhon last year. But it was a different war then. Combat is what you've been trained for and you're all curious to know how you'll do.

You skip supper. The buzzing in your head from the liquor is pleasant and you go up to the flying bridge to watch the sunset. The sea is very calm now. The ship is alone on the ocean and from the bridge you have a clear view in all directions. You are sailing into the sunset and the colors range from pink to scarlet. The clouds stream by; they seem to be moving very fast. You take a cigar and offer one to your friend Jan. You bite the tip off and are just beginning to light it when the ship's intercom crackles, "Now hear this. Now hear this. This is the Captain speaking."

He tells the ship that a Marine landing team has cut off a major Viet Cong force at Van Tuong. They have killed over a thousand of the enemy in the largest United States victory of the war — Operation Starlight. He doesn't have further details.

For a moment there is silence. Then a mighty cheer bursts out — from everywhere aboard the ship there is a voice to be raised. You look at Jan and at the Marines on the decks and you know why you joined the Marine Corps. You don't cheer — because you're an officer. But you feel it, and so does Jan and every other Marine. You wish you'd saved the whiskey to toast the victory. You settle for the sunset — and you dedicate it to those who won.

There are two sailing days left to Okinawa. You will transfer to another ship there and pick up supplies and ammunition for Vietnam. You are anxious for it to begin. This is what you came for.

3
The Initiation

No one sleeps much before his first combat. You're still a virgin. You still have ideals. You're dry and you're safe and your belly is full. You have a lot to be thankful for.

For the first time in your service career no one has to wake you. People start getting up hours before they have to. You take extra care shaving and dressing.

By now most of the troops have developed a certain bravado. They have come to terms with their fear and are practicing Shakespeare's advice about brave men dying but once. Most of them have never read *Julius Caesar*, but that doesn't matter. They are the stuff Shakespeare wrote about.

Steak and eggs is the traditional Marine breakfast before a landing. No one feels much like eating now. Your mouth is dry, and the food tastes like cotton. Lack of sleep and emotional tension are taking their toll. You'll regret not eating in a few hours.

But right now that might as well be in the next century.

You can hear the helicopters warming up on the flight deck. The carrier trembles slightly as she swings into the wind. You know you'll soon be ashore.

By this time everything works automatically. Training has taken over. You go through the prescribed routines you have performed dozens of times. By the numbers. It is just as well. Your mind boggles at what is happening.

In the helicopter you keep thinking what it would be like to get shot. You have never seen combat before and you wonder if it is really like all those briefings you got back in the States and on Okinawa. You remember the officers and men who briefed you on their experiences in Vietnam. They seemed strange — distant. You wonder if you'll become like them.

Suddenly the helicopter is on the ground and you are out of the hatch and running. Your helmet keeps slipping down the side of your head. You're very conscious of the packstraps cutting into your shoulders. The ground feels strange after so long at sea. Your legs are heavy and you can't move as fast as you want to. It's like the childhood nightmare of having to run in slow motion while the neighborhood monster sprints after you at full speed.

Everyone is shouting and pointing and the sand is soft and you can't get a good foothold. You fall down and curse because you are embarrassed. But no one hears. There are strange faces everywhere and you feel lost because they are all doing something.

Your company is setting up a perimeter defense and you begin to recognize faces. For the first time you realize your fear doesn't own you anymore. The familiar faces, the officers looking at their maps, the sergeants yelling, the muffled gunfire in the distance — you are a part of it all. You are suddenly very aware that you have a job to do. And that job is the most important thing in the world at the moment. You know you are being depended on to get it done. And you know you will. You still haven't answered a lot of questions, but they are beginning to answer themselves.

By noon you are a veteran. You haven't been shot at yet, but you know you'll react all right when it comes. And somehow that is more important than being shot at.

No one in your company has been hit yet. You have seen a few bodies wrapped in ponchos being carried back to the CP for evacuation. That is different; you didn't know them.

The company is moving again. Orders have come down to replace Foxtrot Company on a ridgeline for the night. You move into their defensive positions and joke with them about how soft they are — going back to the CP just when things are beginning to get rough.

You check your men's foxholes to make sure they have grenade sumps and that there's room to get all the way down. Your gunnery sergeant comes by and talks about clearing fields of fire. You chop some more brush away from your position.

You realize how very tired you are. And hungry. Steak and eggs is just a dream now. And so is that soft rack back on the ship. The water in your canteen tastes of metal and chlorine, but it's still good.

You begin to relax a little. Someone throws you a C ration. Ham and limas again — but it doesn't matter. They all taste the same at this point.

It will be dark soon, and the man you're sharing your foxhole with — your runner — offers you a cigarette. Your mouth is dry, but you smoke it anyway. You check your magazines to make sure they are all loaded and handy. One of the battalion staff comes by checking positions. He says to get some sleep now because they never attack until after midnight. You ask about casualties, but no one seems to know. You lean back against the parapet and close your eyes.

You open them a month later and find that a couple of hours have gone by and that it's dark now and very cold. The artillery is firing every few minutes, and the muffled explosions sound miles away. One of the destroyers supporting you cuts loose with a salvo at an enemy position. Nothing makes quite the same sound as naval gunfire and you jump in spite of yourself.

A machine gun opens up somewhere off to the right and the night is alive with tracers stitching in all directions. You want to fire, but you can't see anything to shoot at. Your runner is crouching down deep in the foxhole. You realize he is more afraid than you. You feel superior. And you feel responsible. You reach out and touch his shoulder. You smile at him in the dark. He can't see it, but he knows and feels better.

It's quiet again. It must have been a false alarm.

You hear a sentry's challenge in the distance and rifle fire seconds later. For the first time in your life you hear the sharp flat crack of incoming enemy fire. You duck into the hole and when you look up flares are going off. Everything flickers in a nightmare-green glow.

It takes a few moments for your eyes to adjust. You can make out forms in front of your foxhole. You can't tell where the men leave off and the shadows begin. But you're very aware that both are coming at you.

You punch off the safety and point your rifle at the shadows. They are about a hundred meters away. You fire three or four rounds and look to see if you have hit anything. But you don't have time to look; the shadows are closer. You can see tracers and muzzle flashes cutting the night. A shadow is throwing a grenade at a foxhole on your left. You point your rifle and empty the magazine. There is a roar as the explosive goes off. The shadow has vanished.

Your own artillery begins a prepared barrage. The shells are landing less than a quarter of a mile away. The ground shakes as they go off and you are vaguely conscious that your ears hurt. You are yelling something at your runner, but he is too busy firing to pay any attention.

The ground stops trembling and the flares begin

to die. The firing is less and less. There are no more shadows.

Your hand stings. You burned it by holding the barrel of your rifle while you fired it. But that doesn't matter now. You won. They tried to take your ground and you beat them off. Your hand begins to swell and pain throbs through it. It is your badge of honor. You accept the discomfort because it reminds you that you won.

As the pain increases you begin to wonder if any of your buddies got it. Your CO comes by checking on casualties and you want to mention your hand. You wonder if you will get a Purple Heart. You think about the stories they will write in the hometown papers. But your CO tells you the third platoon's position was overrun and you don't feel much like a Purple Heart anymore.

It's a long night. The longest you have ever spent. Nothing more happens. You hear a lot of strange sounds. And once you think you see some more shadows moving toward you. But it's nothing.

Dawn brings more than a new day. It brings a new way of life. As the sun comes up the shadows of the night before become twisted and crumpled caricatures of men sprawled around your area. They look like boys — much younger than you. And the flies come. And the stench. They tried to take your ground. And you won.

You have to bury them. First they are searched, then a bulldozer scoops a shallow trench and your men help to throw them into it.

Your company commander sees your swollen

hand and sends you back to the battalion aid station for treatment. You see some friends who have been wounded. And you see the rows of bodies wrapped in ponchos waiting for helicopters to take them away. The enemy dead don't look so young anymore. They just look like enemy dead. And they can't hurt you now. They can't hurt anyone.

You get a tetanus shot and some salve for your hand. You go back to your position as soon as you're released. You are embarrassed by your hand now. And you feel sick when you look at the bodies — neat in their rows.

You survive the rest of the operation. It's all the same. The fear will always be the same — and the frustration — and the anger — and the sorrow. But you are different. You are aware of it in the helicopter on the way back to the ship. You can't put the feeling into words. You can't explain it and somehow you don't want to.

4
The Welcome

"I sure am glad you people are here to replace us."
The captain spoons another mouthful of ham and
limas from the C ration tin and goes on talking while
he chews.

" 'Course, we haven't had it too bad. It's a quiet
sector. But we've been up here four or five months
now and I got a wife back in the States that's going
to need a new bed when I get there." The captain
is flying home next week.

"You sure you don't want any C's?"

You tell him you aren't hungry.

"This area here," he walks toward a series of
three sandbagged bunkers placed so they can support one another by fire, "is where we had most of
our trouble. It's pretty close to the river and Charlie
floats his people down on rafts every now and then
and tries to jump us."

The captain tosses the empty C ration tin into a
bunker.

"We were going to clear away some fields of fire and set up some outposts here, but with you people moving in and us leaving and all we just never got to it."

He pulls out a pack of C ration cigarettes and stares at it before he rips off the cellophane and takes out a bent and flattened cigarette.

"Smoke?" he asks.

You shake your head. It's too hot to smoke.

"Charlie knows there'll be new troops in the area and he's liable to send some men down here. I'd set up some outposts if I were you. You've got four rifle companies out on the perimeter, but this tactical area of responsibility is so big you could march a division of Chinese between here and the nearest company and no one would ever know." He smiles sadly.

You ask him where the likely infiltration routes from the river are, but he shrugs and says there are at least fifty trails and any of them could be used.

"Let's go back and have a beer and I'll tell you how you can get liquor out of the doggies up at Hue," he says with a grin.

You stop at one of the bunkers and look in. There is a pile of empty C ration tins and ammo boxes in a corner. The sandbags are old and some have rotted and spilled sand in little heaps on the floor of the bunker. You make a note to get them repaired. And you decide that the elephant grass is too high and the vegetation too thick between the bunkers. It will have to be cleared.

You meet with your company staff late in the afternoon. The sun is very hot and you're all sweating heavily. You open the large metal ammo box you use as an ice chest and pass around some cans of beer. The beer is cold and tastes very sharp and good.

You begin the meeting by asking your staff what they found and how it can be improved.

"We didn't find much, lieutenant, and anything we do is bound to improve what's here," your gunnery sergeant says. The rest of your men nod in agreement.

"I don't know what these pogey-bait Marines were doing up here," your supply sergeant says. "The place is a mess. Everything is run-down or broken. The holes aren't deep enough, the sandbags are rotted, half the comm wire is shorted out. They must never have done anything."

"Or they were anxious to get the hell out of here and go home," the first sergeant says.

You tell the gunny to collect a list of all the things that need to be done and that you and he and the first sergeant will get together later and make a priority list of things to do.

"It's our home now," you remind your men. "We've got to live here. I don't care what we've inherited, we'll turn it into something."

There is a loud explosion in the distance, and the ground trembles.

"Jesus Christ! Sounds like incoming."

You and your men sprint for the nearest bunker. There are more explosions — each nearer than the one before. You hear pieces of shrapnel whistle overhead. You dive into the bunker and see the grinning face of the captain who escorted you around the area earlier in the morning.

"Charlie's just saying hello, Lieutenant. Welcome aboard."

5
The Sweep

It is still dark when you reach the phase line and very wet. It rained during the night and even though it stopped hours ago the ground and the foliage are soaked. At the phase line your company will fan out to cover the floor of a valley. At dawn you will sweep the valley — looking for Viet Cong or arms' caches or food stocks. Other rifle companies will sweep the ridges and cover you. Your boots are filled with water and they squeak when you move. It will be light soon. You walk over to your gunnery sergeant.

"Which one's loaded?" you ask him. He always fills one canteen with whiskey and one with water. This is the gunny's third war.

He unsnaps his right canteen and hands it to you.

"I don't like this operation, Lieutenant," he says. "It's too quiet."

"You've been watching too many war movies, Gunny. It's always quiet at 0500."

"But it's different this time. There ain't no birds squawking, or animals, or nothing."

"It's the weather. Nothing makes any noise when it rains."

You take another swig from his canteen and feel the whiskey burn your throat as you drink it. You trace the path of the liquor as it moves toward your belly and you feel warm and good when it hits your stomach.

"Have a drink?" You hand the canteen to your sergeant.

"Thanks, I will."

The floor of the valley you are to move through is about 1200 meters wide. You will sweep it with three platoons abreast and one platoon kept in reserve with you and the command group. You don't really think you'll need a reserve, but you want to be sure. There is a reinforced battalion on this operation and the enemy never stays to fight unless he has you outnumbered. Intelligence reports indicate no more than a company of VC in the area. But intelligence reports have been wrong.

You check your watch and see that it is H hour — time to begin. You pass the word to your platoon leaders, and the company starts to move.

The wet elephant grass brushes against your legs and in a matter of minutes you are dripping. Your platoons have moved out to cover their assigned areas and are moving well. You look over at your gunny, and he shakes his head.

"It wasn't like this in the Old Corps," he says.

The gunny is a small man physically and he keeps

slipping in the mud. Every time he stumbles he curses to himself, but never loudly enough for the troops to hear.

You cut yourself a bamboo walking stick the night before and it helps you keep your balance as you move over the wet field. The gunny laughed at the stick last night. He's not laughing now.

"You ought to join the New Corps, Gunny," you say and wave your stick at him.

He just shakes his head.

It is light now and you can see a village a hundred meters in front of your lead platoon. It's not a village really — just a collection of huts with a couple of water buffalo working the rice paddies.

When the command group reaches the huts, your first platoon is finishing its search. They have found nothing and you look at Captain Binh, head of the Vietnamese interpreter-interrogator team assigned to you.

He shakes his head. "No VC here. Only women and children. We no catch VC today."

This is the first time you have worked with ARVN troops. Binh doesn't seem interested in the operation. You wonder whether all ARVN are like that. You knew some Vietnamese officers while you were at Basic School and they only wanted to eat. They weren't very enthusiastic about the training and most of them stuck together and didn't mix with the other officers.

One of your platoons has sent back some Viet Cong suspects and you turn them over to Binh and his men. The prisoners don't look like much to you — mostly old men and women with a scattering of children. Binh agrees with you, and they are returned to their homes. The ones that are retained are sent to collection points where they will be picked up by helicopters and taken to Phu Bai for more thorough questioning.

You hear a low roar in the distance. It grows steadily louder and you can make out a flight of armed helicopters streaking toward a long ridgeline on your left. You watch as the rockets from the copters stream to the ground. It is several seconds before you hear the sound of the firing.

"Somebody's found VC," you say to Binh and nod at the gunships.

"No VC here," Binh says. "They just play."

You shrug and watch your lead platoons combing the terrain. The sun is well up now and the grass is beginning to dry. But the air is very heavy and you are starting to sweat. The cultivated land is falling behind you — giving way to sandy soil and steeper hills. You notice the gunny taking a drink — from his right canteen. He sees you watching him and grins, "I've joined up, Lieutenant. I've joined the New Corps." He brandishes a freshly cut walking stick, and you both laugh.

You hear firing to your right and see a Vietnamese in black pajamas ducking into a cave halfway up a sandy hill. You watch a Marine run to the cave's mouth and throw a grenade inside. You duck — even though you are well out of range. But nothing happens. Just when you're sure the grenade is a dud you see the whitened head of a very old Vietnamese man emerge from the cave. He is holding the grenade in his hand and walking unsteadily toward the nearest Marine — the man who threw the grenade. He is returning the explosive. The Marine forgot to remove the protective tape from the spoon. Even if the ring is pulled, a grenade won't go off unless the spoon flies free.

You smile in spite of your anger at the Marine's stupidity and you hear the gunny telling a runner to get the Marine and bring him to the command group.

"I'm going back to the Old Corps for a few minutes, Sir." The gunny taps his stick in his free hand.

When you reach a small plateau — the highest point in the valley — you signal your company to take a short break for lunch. You have been moving for hours and you should have let the men rest some time ago. But you wanted to reach the plateau and the going was slower than you expected.

You open a tin of apricots and begin to suck the liquid from the can. You have trouble eating in the field. You think it must be the excitement. You never eat C ration heavies — ham and limas, beans and franks, beef and potatoes. You just like the fruit. And the best part of the meal is the juice.

You have about two miles to go before you reach the end of the valley. Helicopters will pick you up there and return you to Phu Bai. You take off your boots and rub your feet before you give the order to resume the sweep. Your feet are white and wrinkled and have no feeling in them. They don't seem to be a part of you. Two more miles, you think, and you begin to imagine how good a beer is going to taste when you get back to camp.

The valley is getting wider now. It is one of three valleys that empty into a large plain. The plain is a wild tangle of jungle underbrush and trees. No one lives there, and it would take a division a week to search it properly. You are to move to the edge of the plain and signal for helicopters to take you home.

From behind you, you hear the sudden hammering of a machine gun. The bullets crack sharply as they fly past and some make a long whistling sound as they cut the brush. You are yelling for your radioman, but he has been hit and is lying face down in the elephant grass. The bullet that hit him wrecked the radio and you yell for a runner. You tell the runner to get to the reserve platoon and have them envelop the machine gun from the right. You make him repeat the message and he starts to look up — ready to go — when you hear the gunny shouting.

"Cover him, goddam it. Give him covering fire."

You see Captain Binh disappear into the grass, moving quickly and running bent over. You tell your runner to wait. The men in your command group are firing steadily now, taking turns and shooting just enough to keep the enemy gunners from aiming. The VC are firing wildly and you can tell they can't see what they're shooting at.

You crawl through the grass to the gunny. "Where's Binh going?"

"He's going to get himself killed if he keeps this up, Lieutenant. He's gone after the gun. He just said he would go to the right and to give him cover. And then he was gone." The gunny shrugs. "Keep firing, keep firing," he yells.

Suddenly, there is the roar of a grenade going off and the sharp snapping of Binh's submachine gun being fired in long bursts. You and the gunny are on your feet and running toward the enemy gun. You have your pistol in your hand and you chamber a round and ease the hammer down with your thumb. You can see Binh in the distance. He has replaced the clip in his gun and is still firing. Everything else is quiet.

When you reach him he stops firing and stands there with his weapon dangling at his side. There is a foxhole with a camouflaged lid that has been blown off. There are four bodies lying in and around the hole and the grass at the edges of the hole is burnt black and smoking. The bodies have been riddled with bullets.

"Spider trap, Lieutenant," the gunny says. "That first platoon must have walked right over it and then Charlie popped up and started shooting."

Binh stares at the bodies and says something in Vietnamese. You watch as he prods the bodies onto their backs with the toe of his boot — his face impassive.

"We finally got some VC, Captain Binh," you say to him.

"VC," he says, "kill VC." He loads a fresh clip

31

and walks back to the command group.

"He's a tough one," you tell the gunny. "That was a brave thing he did."

"Yes sir, it was. But it was foolish too. He's going to get himself killed doing that. And from what I've seen of the ARVN they can't spare too many like him."

You nod and remember your radioman. "Have somebody search these VC, Gunny. And you better get somebody to take care of the radioman. I'll be calling for choppers to take us home as soon as I get a new radio."

"Aye, aye, sir." The gunny shakes his head. "First there was the Old Corps, then there was the New Corps. And now there's this goddam thing. What's next, Lieutenant?"

"I don't know, Gunny," you shrug. "I just don't know."

6
The Cemetery

R and R means rest and recreation. For those lucky enough to get an R and R flight out of Vietnam it means a lot more. It's sleeping in a bed with sheets. It's having a hot shower and getting really clean. It's getting up whenever you want to. It's having a cold beer. It's not getting shot at — for a few days.

Manila is a pretty quiet R and R town compared to Hong Kong or Bangkok or Tokyo. But when they offer you R and R you take it. It doesn't matter where. Tokyo would be available in a couple of weeks. But in Vietnam two weeks is often a lifetime.

The battalion had been on two operations in the past month. At Vung Mu you had been bloodied. And at Tam Quan you engaged a battalion of the People's Army of North Vietnam. You'll always remember Tam Quan and how the enemy drove a herd of water buffalo and some women and old men at your positions. They hoped you would be too soft to fire through them at the soldiers running behind. You weren't soft. And you remember the rice paddy water was red for days afterward. And you remember the screams of the wounded and the dying. And your men sweating and cursing and firing and bleeding underneath the hot Vietnamese sun. And the taste of fear in your mouth when some enemy soldiers broke through your lines. And you remember having to bury the dead and clean the wounded and tell the living there would be more and it would be worse. And the sick feeling in your stomach when they brought your friend Red back in a poncho for his final flight home. You had been in the same platoon at Officers' Candidate School. You thought of the time you went AWOL together to Washington, D.C., because there had been no liberty that weekend. They never caught you.

You don't wait for Tokyo or Bangkok or Hong Kong. You go to Manila.

As the plane leaves the runway at Da Nang you feel a tremendous sense of relief. You think about your troops — who haven't gotten any R and R — and you're sorry for them. You tell yourself that your staying wouldn't have helped them get R and R, that you might as well enjoy it while you can, that you'll be back in the field soon enough.

The plane takes sniper fire as it rises from Da Nang and heads toward the sea. Even after weeks of getting shot at you flinch and duck.

You try to sleep as the plane drones east to the Philippines. You spent several months at Subic Bay the year before and you know the Islands and the people. You'd have liked Japan better, but Manila will do. You want to have a good time and that means spending money. Bars and girls are expensive in the Philippines. What money you don't drink up you're determined to bet at the cock fights in Quezon City.

As the plane circles Manila, a naval officer points out Bataan and Corregidor. But you don't look. You have seen Bataans and Corregidors by other names — and they all look the same.

You change into civilian clothes at the airport and pick up a ride into downtown Manila. You are with another officer from your battalion and you check into the Manila Hotel.

You go straight to the tub and fill it with hot, soapy water. Jack comes back with a dozen bottles of iced San Miguel beer. It doesn't matter that you won't drink them all. You turn up the air conditioner as high as it will go and sit there drinking and telling each other how lucky you are to get away.

You drink three or four beers apiece and decide to go out and see the town. It hasn't changed much since you saw it last a year before. It's the same sunswept city with the same chattering people.

It is very hot and as you begin to sweat you regret drinking so much. Jack suggests you solve this problem by sampling some more of the local brew. You pick a place that advertises "the coldest beer in the Far East." It is and so are the girls. But that doesn't matter now. You are still enjoying your freedom.

You suddenly remember crouching in a trench

near a village as enemy fire whistled and cracked overhead. You had been pinned down for nearly an hour. And while you waited for air strikes to relieve the pressure, elements from an advance platoon were moving back to the trench line. One man was running — low and ducked over — trying to use the huts for cover. He didn't make it. An enemy .50 caliber machine gun hit him in the stomach and he leaned back against one of the huts, holding his intestines in his hands and slowly sinking to the ground. Before you could say anything a corporal dropped his pack and sprang over the parapet toward the wounded man. He had only gotten a few feet when an enemy bullet slammed into his arm and knocked him down. You watched as he pulled himself up and started for the man again. He got all the way to the hut before a .50 hit him in the shoulder and spun him down. His squad leader was yelling for him to stay down. But he didn't know how. After what seemed a very long time he pulled himself up and was reaching for his wounded comrade when another .50 slammed through his chest and he died.

Like a couple of children turned loose in a candy store you and Jack sample everything you can. And move on to sample some more.

You buy a monkeypod salad bowl for some friends back home. The souvenir shops are all pretty much the same. Monkeypod (acacia wood) is the specialty of the Islands and you can get it carved in any shape or design you want. You choose a couple of wooden water buffalo and think about buying a large Marine emblem they have hanging in the back of the store. But you don't have much room to hang things in your tent in Vietnam. You pay for your souvenirs and you and Jack go to the Army-Navy Club to get them wrapped and mailed.

The Army-Navy Club resembles the old British clubs in India. There is no air conditioning, but the Club sits at the edge of Manila Bay and there's always a breeze. The ceilings are about three stories high and punkahs (large fans) keep the air circulating. And there's always someone ready to take your order for a drink. You and Jack sit on the veranda and drink gin-and-tonics and watch the sun sink toward the bay. The only sound is the faint rustle of leaves in the banyan trees and the squeak of a punkah that needs oil. You drink a lot and don't say much.

A thousand miles to the west they will be sending out ambush patrols for the night and rigging booby traps and establishing listening posts. Men will be checking their weapons to make sure that dirt and sand and mud won't clog them when they are needed. They will be stripping the protective tape from the spoons of hand grenades. They will be having their last smoke before the morning. They will be joking and writing letters. They will be thinking and talking quietly to each other. They will be staring into the thickening jungle gloom. And some of them will be dying.

You decide to drive out to Fort Bonifacio and see the American cemetery there before it gets too dark. The taxi takes you through a section of Manila you have never seen before. It could be Westchester or Winnetka or Bel Air. The homes are beautiful and spacious and well kept. The gardens and lawns sparkle with tropical flowers in the late afternoon sun.

You pass through the gate at Fort Bonifacio just before they secure it for the night. You drive along a winding road up the hill to the cemetery.

You had been to the Tomb of the Unknown Soldier at Arlington and the Punchbowl in Hawaii and Cemetery Ridge at Gettysburg. But they were just places. Places that stirred boyish visions of charging horses and flashing sabers and rattling musketry — of honor and heroes and glory. You looked at their crosses and thought of the living — of yourself. At Fort Bonifacio you look at the crosses and think of the dead. And you think of Vietnam.

You think of your grandfather — who fought in the Philippines at the turn of the century. And of your father and uncles who had come through here in World War II. You think of all the Americans who had come through, and here at twilight of those who stayed.

Jack goes up to the main chapel. You walk alone through the rows of crosses, pausing every now and then to straighten a clump of grass or clod of earth that seems out of place.

You wander — not really looking for anything in particular — just reading the names and ranks and dates on the crosses. At the end of one of the rows you find yourself staring at a cross. Suddenly, you realize the name on the cross is your own.

You want to run and show the cross to Jack. You want to heap it with flowers. You want to cry out that this one — that bears your family name — is special. But there is probably one there with Jack's name too. And a floral wreath would wither in a few days. And no grave is special — only the people in them.

You walk very slowly up a flagstone path to the main memorial and join Jack. Two crescent archways meet at a small chapel. The columns supporting the crescents bear the names of all those Americans who died in and for the Philippines in World War II. There are mosaics of state seals and mosaics depicting major battles in the Pacific. Your steps echo sharply as you walk to the chapel. You buy some candles and light them and place them in the iron holders near the door.

When it is too dark to see the white crosses anymore you go back to your cab. You don't speak. The driver asks softly if you have found the names of your relatives. Yes, you tell him, but he wouldn't understand.

You go to the most expensive restaurant in Manila for dinner — the Madrid. You keep thinking of olive-drab tins of C rations as the table is set with silver and linen and crystal. You order steaks and the wine helps to brighten your mood. Jack buys a couple of Tabacalera cigars and over coffee you talk about where you will go after dinner. You mention several bars you know of from past experience — Pauline's, the Club Oro, the East Inn — and you talk of the girls you have known — Esther, Big Ida, Norma.

Then, as if you have no control over your own voice, you tell Jack you're going to catch the plane back the next day. "I know," he says, "I know."

It is different coming into Vietnam this time — maybe because you have chosen to return. You and Jack arrange for a jeep to take you back to your outfit. The sergeant at the flight terminal keeps shaking his head. He can't understand why you returned five days early. Neither can you.

Strange war. But then you've never known any other war.

7

The Prisoners

The Viet Cong prisoners sit against the hut. It is an old mud-walled hut, and bits of straw stick out from it where it is beginning to crack. It is hot and though the wind blows hard it offers no relief.

Two Marine sentries sit on empty water cans at each end of the hut and watch the prisoners with casual interest. They are discussing their last liberty in Da Nang and one of them is talking about a girl they'd both known.

The other laughs and stands up slowly. The water can topples in the dust, and the enemy soldiers look first at the can and then at the Marine.

There are five prisoners squatting against the hut. They have been stripped naked and are sitting silently a few meters apart. They remain impassive as one Marine flicks his cigarette away, clicks off the safety, and swings the muzzle of his rifle at them.

"Don't get too comfortable, gook," he says and

fires a round into the hut above their heads.

There is a solid smack as the bullet hits the wall, and a puff of dried mud showers the Vietnamese. They don't look too comfortable.

"Christ's sake, don't do that," the other sentry says. "Now we'll have the lieutenant over here."

"Got to keep them in shock," the shooter replies. "That's what the book says."

"But you know what the lieutenant says."

"Hell, who cares. Besides, the one on the end looked like he was going to run."

"The hell he did."

"But the lieutenant don't know that, Peters."

"No, I guess not."

You have heard most of the dialogue and seen what happened. But one of your superiors is certain to ask about it, and you'll have to tell him something. So you walk over to the guards to hear their explanation.

The sentries see you coming and stand up as you approach.

"The one on the end looked like he was going to make it, sir," the shooter says.

The other sentry nods.

You know what has happened. The sentries haven't been in Vietnam very long, but you don't bother to question them further. You think to yourself that you'd better get them reassigned before they kill one of the prisoners.

"Hello, *Dai Wi*," you greet Captain Binh, the Vietnamese interpreter attached to your battalion. Binh had been with you a few weeks earlier on a sweep near Que Son, and he earned your respect by enveloping an enemy machine gun alone and killing four Viet Cong. Binh is a good soldier. But like good soldiers who have played at war too long, he also likes to kill.

Binh pulls out a pack of Gauloises and offers you one. You take it and light his cigarette and then your own. Binh inhales deeply and blows the smoke toward the sky.

"Who shoot?" he asks.

"One of my sentries wants to shoot your VC," you say and smile.

"Good idea," Binh smiles too. "Why you don't kill VC?"

"They're prisoners," you tell him.

"The VC kill eight — ten — of your men today," Binh says and waves his arm toward the prisoners. "Why you don't kill them?"

You shake your head. You and Binh have had this discussion before.

Binh looks at you and says, "We wear same uniform, but we different men."

He crushes his Gauloise against a palm tree and takes a step as if to depart. He hesitates and looks back. "You learn," he says, "you learn." And he moves off to the S-2 tent.

Late in the afternoon one of the rifle companies sends back three more prisoners. Two of the prisoners are women. They are very old and wrinkled and they walk hunched over. Their mouths are stained a reddish brown from years of chewing betel nut. One of the women is yelling something at the

Marine guard who prods her along. A Vietnamese interpreter-interrogater hits the old woman in the face hard with his closed fist and she stops yelling.

You tell the battalion intelligence officer that Golf Company has sent back more Viet Cong suspects and then tell your company gunnery sergeant to post another sentry. You want the women segregated from the men and you tell one of the sentries to make sure they keep them separated.

"Can we strip the women too, Lieutenant?" one of the sentries asks.

"Save it for Da Nang, Peters."

"I go for that old stuff, sir."

"You don't need to strip the women. Just search them."

When Captain Binh returns to the battalion area he takes two of his interrogator team to the compound to question the prisoners.

Binh starts with the men, and it isn't pretty to watch. All the talking is in Vietnamese, but screams don't need translation. Binh and his men take a prisoner out of sight of his fellows, but not out of earshot. They ask the prisoner questions and beat him about the face and head with stout bamboos when they don't get the answer they want. After a few minutes they return the used prisoner and start on another. The bamboo doesn't break bones, but it leaves welts and the prisoners' faces are badly swollen when they are returned.

The women are quiet during the beatings and they watch with apparent resignation as their turns approach. When Binh approaches the women and motions, one of them — the older — gets up very slowly. As she stands she pulls a hand grenade from under her coarse peasant's *ao dai* and pushes it at Binh. There isn't time to do anything but watch Binh and the old woman dissolve in a hail of shrapnel. The sentries and Binh's men empty their automatic rifles into the remaining prisoners and the noise is deafening.

The old woman was able to kill Binh because you hadn't stripped her. If you had stripped her, Binh would be alive now — and so would the prisoners. You are sick. You are embarrassed and you feel ashamed.

As you turn toward the CP and start to walk back you remember Binh's words. "You learn," he had said. And you think of the drinking song the troops sing and of the last lines:

"We're using a theory, we've used it before; If you ain't got no people, you ain't got no war."

8
The Wounded

Blood is the currency of war. It's just like money really. You try to invest yours — to get as high a return as possible. And you try to spend the enemy's. But, unlike money, war doesn't require any fancy conversion tables. You can figure your investment with something as simple as a life. In Vietnam the field aid station is one of the places where the results of the investment are measured. And the field aid station is where you go to visit two of your wounded men.

You don't like hospitals very much. It probably started when you were very young and you watched your mother die in one. You remember the strong chemical smells and the scrubbed look of the nurses and doctors. You remember how busy everyone was and the bells ringing softly and calling away one doctor after another. You remember how clean and bright the sheets were and how tired and gray your mother's face looked against the pillow. That may have started it, but the field aid station has added something of its own.

If a battle has been going on for a long time, the aid stations literally run with blood. After a while you can recognize when a stain was made by its color and smell. If a stain is very old — a week — it is dark brown and only smells faintly. The fresher it is the brighter it is — and the more it smells. You can't really describe the smell. You can say that it's sweet and sickly and sharp. You can say that it makes you gag and want to vomit. You can say it smells like many things. And it does. But you can't describe it. You have to experience it.

You notice the brown stain on the tent flap that serves as a door for the aid station. You can barely see it and you decide that the stain must be very old. A doctor in an olive-drab jacket looks up from a pile of papers he is sifting through and you ask him where you can find two men from your unit who have been wounded and brought here for treatment. He checks a roster and gives you the tent number and says they plan to evacuate one of the men to the Philippines later in the day. You ask him how they are and he unbuttons his jacket pocket and takes out a pipe and some tobacco. He begins to fill the pipe and he gives you that special look all doctors must learn to pass their first year at medical school — the look they reserve for those times a non-doctor asks so foolish and unanswerable a question as how a patient is. You recognize the look and don't wait to hear the second-year medical school reply.

You find the tent your men are in and scrape the mud from your boots before you go in. The tent smells heavily of canvas and rubbing alcohol, but the flaps have been rolled up and the air moves freely. There is a corpsman sleeping on a cot at the far end of the tent. You suppose there must be a regulation about checking in with him, but you see your men and walk quickly to their cots.

One of them — a staff sergeant — was blinded by shrapnel from a short artillery round. They don't know how serious it is and he will be sent to Clark Field in the Philippines for further examination. His head has been wrapped with several layers of gauze bandages and looks grotesquely out of proportion. You whisper a greeting to him and take his hand and shake it and tell him you wanted to see him before they flew him out. He laughs and says that he'd like to be able to see his departure. You feel his hand trembling and you realize you have been holding it and you release it.

Your other man is a corporal who was wounded in the arm. The bullet went in about six inches above his elbow and came out the other side. The corporal has no feeling in the arm. He asks you how things are going back at the unit and says he wishes he were back there with you. You tell him that he's better off where he is — especially with all his pretty nurses. The wounded man looks toward the sleeping corpsman and shakes his head sadly.

"That stupid swabbie ain't even a sailor, Lieutenant, let alone a nurse."

"You'll be back with some real nurses soon," you

tell him. You know they can't treat nerve damage in Vietnam and that they will probably send him to the naval hospital on Guam when they decide that he isn't faking and that there is nothing more they can do for him at the aid station.

You ask the sergeant if he needs anything. You tell him they are going to fly him to the Philippines later and that the clerks back at the unit have packed up his things and will ship them to him as soon as he gets settled. He asks about shaving gear. You say that the Red Cross people who will meet his plane at Clark will give him all he needs. He shakes his head and says the only other thing he needs is a new pair of eyes. You tell him not to give up on the pair that he has.

You talk with your men about the weather and how the food is and what is going on back at your unit. You tell them what happened during the operation after they were wounded. You tell them you killed more of the enemy than you actually did because you know it will make them feel good and you only have to lie a little to make it sound like a major victory. You get them to talk about their wives back home and you know they are feeling better now.

A corpsman comes into the tent and tells the sergeant that they have to get him ready for an air-evac to Clark and you tell both of your men that it's time for you to go. You shake hands with them and joke again with the corporal about the nurses. You pass the doctor's tent on the way to your jeep and you can smell his pipe tobacco. It seems strange and foreign after the canvas and alcohol.

In the jeep on the way back to your outfit you hear the roar of a transport plane and you look up and watch it heading eastward toward the sea. You wonder if the sergeant is on it and you think what it must be like to be blind. But you can't afford to think about that for very long and you force it out of your mind and stare at the twisted dirt road carrying you back to your unit and to war.

9
The Patrol

There are many ways of getting on a patrol. You can be on a regular rotation list. Or you can volunteer. Or your CO can pick you because he doesn't like you. Or you can just happen to be near the operations tent when a mission comes up. But one thing remains the same — if you go looking for trouble long enough you're bound to find it. And you only hope you're ready when it comes.

You don't know why you walk past the operations tent. You know what it can lead to. But you're bored with filing service record books and checking defensive positions and signing casualty reports. You tell yourself you're going to the Lister bag for water, but you don't believe it.

An hour later you have a patrol — and a mission. There are three kinds of patrols. On a reconnaissance patrol you look for information — and try not to be seen. On an ambush patrol you establish a position — and wait for an enemy who seldom comes. On a combat patrol you look for the enemy — and try to kill him. You have a combat patrol.

You were in the area the patrol is to move through several weeks earlier on a battalion sweep. It is rugged terrain with hills hundreds of meters high. There are sudden drops from the trails. The jungle canopy blots out the sun and makes the trails hot, damp tunnels forever shrouded in half-light and shadows. There are many good ambush sites for the enemy. But because it's bad and because no one has tried it before and because you have a Nung guide, a Chinese mercenary, you have a chance — if you depend on surprise, and luck.

You have to walk in. It will take about two days. Helicopters could get you there in minutes. But they would sacrifice surprise. They will be standing by for medical evacuations.

You only have a few hours to ready the patrol — so elaborate preparations and rehearsals are out. You check your equipment. There will be little demolition work so there's no need to carry satchel charges and plastic explosives. You will carry extra ammunition instead. But you don't want to burden your men with excess gear. You have a long way to go and you have to be prepared to move fast. You will wear soft caps and jungle uniforms instead of helmets and flak jackets. You check your men and brief them and joke with them. And you hope the war will be over before you leave.

You and your men have been at Vung Mu together. And at Tam Quan. And Phu Thu. And Que

Son. And a thousand nameless places. Places where you knew fear and suffering and death. And a thousand more where you knew courage and hope and victory. There is a bond between you.

You feel lost when you leave your lines on a mission. It doesn't matter how often you do it — it's always the same. You're leaving something safe — something secure — for a few hours or days or perhaps forever. The men in your outposts don't like to look at you as you pass. You're dead men to them — until you return.

Your radioman whispers the call signal even though you're only minutes outside your lines.

It's a hot day. The monsoons are months away. Your mind begins to wander in spite of your efforts to concentrate on the things you have to do as patrol leader. The soles of your feet sting as the heat from the ground works through your boots. You remember driving across America as a boy with your family. You remember stopping in the New Mexico desert at a little drugstore and hearing your father order limeades for everyone. You'd never had a limeade before and you remember the waitress squeezing some tiny green limes by hand. The drink was tart and cold and refreshing. It made you feel very cool and you wish you had one now. You pull one of your canteens from its pouch and take a deep draught. It's still cool and it's a lot better than the paddy water you'll be drinking in a few hours.

Your Nung guide speaks very little English, but he has worked with Americans before and he understands the hand and arm signals you worked out at the CP. He is taller than the Vietnamese and with his shaven head he looks like a Malay pirate. He walks on the balls of his feet and is very quiet and watchful. You decide he won't give you away. But you keep your eye on him.

By the first nightfall you have come almost twelve miles. You move your patrol off the trail and up a little finger of ground. You have them fan out into a 360-degree perimeter for the night. No fires are allowed. Smoke could give your position away. There is no talking. You designate a brief time for opening C rations and eating. The cans will be buried in the morning.

After you have whispered your instructions to the squad leaders you settle down. It is still hot and will be all night. There is nothing to do but endure it. You keep thinking of that limeade.

Everyone is ready to go before first light. No one has slept very much. You finish the last of your G.I. water. You motion to your squad leaders to have someone collect canteens and fill them in the stream near the ridge. They will have to last the day.

It doesn't take long to work out the night's stiffness. Everyone is watchful now and alert. A monkey sits in a coconut palm watching the patrol struggle up a jungle trail. He seems fascinated. You look back to note how many of the men have seen the monkey. Most of them have. That's a good sign.

Your point man freezes and the patrol halts. You hear safeties clicking off and you move forward to see what the trouble is. The trail empties into a small clearing and there are three or four huts standing on the far side. A water buffalo grazes at the edge of the clearing and some women and children thresh rice in front of one of the huts. You look at the Nung and he nods — it is all right. You tell two scouts to take the Nung and search the area. They understand; they will kill the Nung if there is an ambush.

You watch them move through the clearing and toward the huts. The water buffalo snorts and continues to graze. The women look up and seem terrified. It is bad for them to know you are here. Your men disappear into the huts and into the surrounding bush. In a few minutes they signal all clear. The Nung is nodding — they are friendly.

Your patrol moves through the clearing and is swallowed up by the jungle again. It is very hot now — well over 100 degrees. You begin to feel dizzy, but you look at the ground and force yourself to walk ahead. By late afternoon you can hardly see anymore. The sweat drops into your eyes and stings them as fast as you mop your brow. Your clothes are soaked and they cling to your body and scrape it raw. You halt the patrol and have the corpsman issue salt tablets to the men. The Nung isn't sweating at all. He just hunkers down and grins.

Some of your men have been sick. You feel sick yourself. But you know you are close to your staging area and you want to reach it by nightfall. The troops can rest there.

A staging area should be close enough to the enemy to move to the attack quickly. But the area must be secure enough to allow the final preparations for combat. The map indicates such a position about six hundred meters from the enemy base camp. You want to move to an attack position at night and attack at dawn.

You reach your staging area just at dusk. The men are too tired to eat. They just lie down and go to sleep. After posting sentries, you take your squad leaders and the Nung and move off to recon the guerrilla camp.

The camp sits at the juncture of two streams. The streams form a waterfall and the noise of the water masks the sounds of the enemy. It will mask your approach as well. From a rise overlooking the camp you can see the enemy preparing their meal. A small group is washing clothes in one of the streams. You can see an enemy sentry upstream. He is dozing and his head keeps nodding and jerking.

It took you less than an hour to move from your staging area to where you will assault the camp. You think you will be able to move your troops in about three hours. You will let them rest until midnight and then you'll move the final distance.

You decide that the final distance will be easier if you move your men through the jungle to a position between the enemy sentry and the base camp. You can walk the rest of the way in the stream. The stream is about three meters wide and a meter deep. The rush of the water will drown the sounds of your approach. The Nung can have the sentry.

Your plan is to set up a base of fire with one

squad at the southern end of the camp. After they have poured fire through the camp for about thirty seconds, you will launch an assault wave composed of the rest of the platoon. You will place a couple of fire teams to cover your attack and pick off enemy stragglers.

You wake your squad leaders at midnight and have them prepare their men. You are anxious to get it over with. You are too tired to think about casualties or ambushes or traps. The mission is the only thing that matters. You have your plan and you will not change it. You have no imagination left to think up a new one.

Moving at night is always slow. And this close to the enemy it is slower than usual. The terrain is rough, and you have to concentrate all your efforts on it. You forget about the enemy for a while. But at every snapping branch you remember why you're here. By this time you are committed. Your memories of the mutilated bodies of captured Marines, your thoughts of home, your desire to do your job — all are lost in the simple logic that after this operation is over you will rest. One way or another.

The night is so dark you have to maintain physical contact between the men or the column will be broken. You can hear the stream in the distance and you think about the enemy sentry. The water is very cold when you reach the stream. After walking in it for a short while your feet grow numb and you seem very clumsy trying to feel your way along.

You smell the base camp before you see a smoldering cooking fire and the outline of some huts framed against the night sky. All the enemy appear to be asleep. You halt the patrol and your squad leaders take their men to the preplanned positions. There is nothing to do now but wait until dawn — about an hour away.

You don't think during that hour. You enjoy the feeling of the ground as you press yourself against the stream bank. You turn your mind off — perhaps because you're too tired to do anything else. Perhaps because you don't want to think about what you'll be doing in a few minutes.

There is a stirring in the enemy camp and you realize you have been dozing. You curse yourself and look at your watch. It is ten minutes past BMNT (begin morning nautical twilight) — it is first light. The guerrilla base camp is a maze of shadows and huts — all the grayish color of the early morning. You are with the base of fire and the signal for the attack is to be the firing of your automatic rifle. You notice some of your men looking at you and you nod at them and push off the safety.

You pick a hut on the extreme left of the camp and rest it on the front sight blade of your rifle. You press the trigger and squeeze off a long burst. The hut shivers and pieces of it fly off at all angles.

The morning explodes with the deafening stutter of automatic rifle fire. Enemy soldiers fall out of their huts and run a few steps before a burst cuts them down. Someone has kicked over a pen of chickens and they are flapping about adding their presence to the chaos.

The base of fire pours forty rounds apiece into

the camp, and when you throw a red smoke grenade they stop. It takes about thirty seconds to fire six thousand rounds. Now it's up to the assault wave.

The assault wave moves through the camp quickly. The men check each hut after throwing a grenade into it. There is the occasional crackle of rifle fire as one of the perimeter fire teams catches a guerrilla trying to slip away.

In less than five minutes there are no more guerrillas — there are no more huts — there is no more firing. The camp smells of smoke and gunpowder and death.

Your troops drag the enemy bodies into a row and you photograph them for intelligence purposes. The bodies are searched for maps and papers. They won't need them now.

The Nung slips quietly up to your side, grinning, and you remember the enemy sentry. He shows you a small Chinese carbine the VC like to carry. You don't have to worry about the sentry.

At last you can call for helicopters to take you back to the battalion area. And to rest. You have taken three casualties — none serious. One man stepped into a *punji* trap and tore his leg and foot. The others were wounded by their own grenade fragments. There are eighteen enemy dead.

You find a rice cache and pour it into the stream. The little waterfall is beautiful — even on this morning. The sun is beginning to come through the morning grayness and the light sparkles in the dancing water. You burn what is left of the huts and throw tear gas down some escape tunnel entrances.

But nothing comes out. You leave the enemy dead behind. You don't have time to bury them and they will have a good effect on their compatriots. They won't be quite as sure of their safety anymore. They won't be as good soldiers for their worrying.

You walk about a mile to a clearing and set up a defensive perimeter to cover the approaching helicopters. In an hour you are back at the battalion CP for debriefing. There is hot food for everyone — and showers — and rest. As you tick off the events of the past two days for the debriefing officers, your mind can't focus on any of them for very long. It's like the sunlight dancing on that waterfall. Things are fragmented — disjointed.

You remember the heat and the weariness and the sun. And the look on the peasants' faces. And the hut resting on your front sight. And the chickens flapping. And you remember the waterfall. As you close your eyes in the tent you are thankful for these bridges. And for the sleep that makes the bridges unnecessary.

10
The Waitress

The Vietnamese guard knows you and grins and nods as he salutes. You return his salute and walk across the dusty courtyard of the compound to the MACV (Military Assistance Command Vietnam) hotel. The hotel houses the mess. The U.S. Army runs the hotel and they use Vietnamese nationals as cooks so army personnel can collect a special living allowance. But the cooks never eat what they prepare and the food is bad. They seldom serve meat dishes and you don't feel like rice or beans or spaghetti. You were up all night debriefing an ambushed patrol and it's a hot day and very humid — the kind of day you often get in Hue. You wouldn't bother coming in at all, but you have to talk to Tam.

You go to the section of the mess reserved for junior officers. You pick a table in the corner and sit with your back to the wall. It's early and you are the only one there. They won't start serving for half an hour. You open your shirt pocket and take out a letter from a girlfriend in the States. The letter is two weeks old. You save it because it reminds you there is another world. You begin to read the letter when you hear a plate crash in the kitchen. One of the cooks begins shouting in Vietnamese. The room floods with a singsong of high-pitched tones spoken too rapidly for you to note anything but anger.

The door to the kitchen opens and Tam, the waitress, floats across the mess toward your table. A strong odor of stale grease and burnt food escapes before a coiled spring closes the door. It's hard to forget the war in Vietnam — even for a little while. But it's possible when you watch Tam.

You have been in Hue two weeks as the Marine liaison officer with the First ARVN Division headquartered there. You have spent all your free time with Tam. You have orders to return to your outfit at Phu Bai tomorrow. But you told Tam you were posted to Hue permanently. Now it's about to end, and you must tell her the truth. You tried to tell her a couple of days ago, but the words wouldn't come. When you tell her the truth all pretense that it can never end must end as well.

She smiles shyly and waits for you to greet her. You reach out and take her hand. She trembles slightly and pulls back.

"What will other girls say?" she asks.

"Who cares." You don't. But it's very different for her — a Vietnamese. Girls from the better families don't indulge in public displays. She smiles and whispers, "Tonight."

You smile back and tell her not to bring you any lunch, that you're not hungry. You ask her if she needs anything from the PX and you tell her you'll meet her at her place after work. You watch her walk back to the kitchen and when the door closes you get up and leave.

There isn't much you can say to most Vietnamese girls. Language is a barrier. And without language, communication limits itself to hand and arm signals and perhaps looks. Even the bar girls — they speak the best English — are only temporary relief. You still hope — each time a B-girl asks you to buy her a drink — that it will be different this time. But it never is. You think about that as you wait for Tam in front of her house in the Catholic district.

You run your hand over the pasteboard wall, but you're careful not to press too hard. You're afraid the wall will break. It has already begun to crumble at one of the corners, and you don't think it will last through the rainy season. You spoke to an army supply sergeant about getting more pasteboard, but he hasn't been able to find any yet. You stare at the strange shadows the heavy tile roof makes in the fading daylight and you wonder how the walls support it. You like the roof. The tile gives it a permanence you miss very much in most things Vietnamese.

You feel something brush against your arm. You are startled and you jump.

"Chao ông, Trang Wi," Tam says. Hello, Lieutenant.

You take her by the arm and when you're inside

the house you kiss her very hard on the mouth. You feel her trembling in your arms and you suddenly think how very small and delicate she is — like a little girl.

"Let's go to Nguyen's — by the river," you tell her. It was the first place she took you in Hue — a little restaurant on the Perfume River. You haven't been back since that night.

You have to be off the streets by 2400 — midnight — or the MP's and the *Quang Chan* — ARVN MP's — will pick you up for breaking curfew. The only other problem is the occasional terrorist grenade. But if you travel by pedicab, you can pull the canopy over far enough so that no one will recognize you. It's a small risk, you think, and worth it.

The street outside Tam's was paved once, but it hasn't been repaired since the end of World War II. You feel the rocks and broken concrete crunching under your shoes as you walk to the square where the pedicabs wait for passengers.

The cab takes you along the bank of the river. The river is low now, before the rains, but it still moves quickly and looks very pretty from the cab. You pass groups of Vietnamese walking near the river to enjoy its breezes. But they don't notice you. The night smells of cooking rice and *nuoc mam* and the river. The driver stops in front of Nguyen's, and you count out his fare in piastres and give him a small tip.

The restaurant is made of wood and sits on heavy teak pilings driven into the shore and the river bed.

It may have been painted at one time, but that was long ago. From your table in the corner you can watch the river swirling underneath you. You drink a Beer La Rue and watch the waiters sitting near the door talking softly. You and Tam are the only customers tonight.

Tam sees you watching the waiters and says, "You like Vietnamese?"

You look at her and raise your eyebrows before you nod.

"But you not understand war, really, Trang Wi."

You stare at her.

"You like Vietnamese, but you kill them. You not understand what it like for Americans to kill Vietnamese," she continues.

"What is it like for a Vietnamese to kill an American?" you ask.

She shakes her head. "That different. This is Vietnam."

Thank God for that, you think to yourself. "But there would be no Vietnam if the Americans weren't here," you tell her. "What would you — a Catholic — do if the Viet Cong ran things?"

She lowers her eyes and looks into her cup of tea. "I know you are right," she says softly, "but you still not understand."

The waiter brings your dinner. The soup is made from creamed asparagus and chicken feet. If you forget the chicken feet the soup is smooth and good. Most Vietnamese find the feet the best part of the soup and spend minutes savoring them. Tam defers to humor you, although it doesn't really bother you.

65

You each have prawns and a small bowl of steamed rice. You drink another bottle of beer. From your window you can look across the river at a water tower the French built years ago on the outskirts of the old imperial city. It looks stark and surreal in the twilight. The moon is already up and very bright. You watch its reflections riding the currents below you. You have to tell Tam tonight.

It is very quiet in the cab on the way back to her house. It is dark now and you don't bother to put the canopy up. Tam fixes you a cup of tea, and you sit on the edge of the bed and drink it. It is hot and very strong and it makes your nose tickle. You like it and the taste it leaves in your mouth after you drink it is sharp and good.

"You have pictures?" she asks. You open your wallet and take out some snapshots that your family sent from home. Tam likes the pictures and likes to hear you tell of your family in America and your house with its many rooms and your car. You give her the photographs and lean back on the bed. The ceiling is very clean. Tam doesn't share the Vietnamese acceptance of dirt.

When she returns the pictures you take her hand and draw her down beside you on the bed. You tell her that you have orders back to your outfit and that you must leave Hue tomorrow. You tell her you just found out today and there is no way to change them.

She doesn't say anything. You think she will cry, but she doesn't. She is strong. You tell her you can't spend the night with her, that you have to be back at the MACV compound to leave before the curfew is over for the night. You tell her how very sorry you are that it is over — that it ever had to end. You tell her you will write to her when you get back and that you always want to stay in touch with her — no matter what happens to Vietnam. You give her a hundred dollars worth of pure gold. You bought it for her earlier in the day from a Vietnamese jeweler near the compound. It is worth ten thousand piastres at the current exchange rate and you know she can get twice that if she knows where to trade. You can't really buy your way out, you know. But this helps.

You go to the door. You hold her and kiss her and feel her tears wet on your face.

"I won't forget," you tell her. "I won't forget."

You shut the door and walk quickly down the street into the Vietnamese night.

11
The Medal

You kick the dried mud from your boots and pull aside the door flap of your tent. It is very dark inside and smells musty. You drop your pack on the cot. You have worn the pack so long that you feel strange — free and light — without it. You roll up the sides of the tent and tie them to the wooden frame with strips of canvas. It is a ragged job and looks very unmilitary, but there is a breeze blowing and the moving air is cool. It feels good for an operation to end — even a bad one, even one that cost several men, even one you'll remember for many nights to come.

You aren't supposed to write a man up for a medal when he does his job. Everyone is supposed to do his job. But when enemy mortars splash you with hot metal and enemy machine guns spray you with fire you add something to just doing your job. There's more than heat and fatigue and thirst to overcome. You can experience that on a training maneuver. In combat there is fear, the kind of fear that turns your bowels to water. The kind that paralyzes you and at the same time cries for you to run. The kind that makes the heat and the fatigue and the thirst insignificant. When a man does his job with this fear tearing at him — then he rates a medal.

You take a pad of lined yellow paper and a pencil stub from your footlocker. You untie your boots, kick them off, and set them under your cot. You take a cigar from your pocket. This is the last of a box of Tabacaleras you bought in the Philippines. You smell the cigar and roll it in your mouth. You take out your pocketknife and begin to whittle the pencil point sharp. You don't want to start writing.

When you lose men you always remember — and you always think it's your fault — that if you'd done things a bit differently your men would be alive.

You write the name of your corpsman at the top of the page. You write Silver Star next to it. Your clerks can put it all in the right form. You think how the clerks always stay behind and a sudden shock of anger overwhelms you. But they just do their job. Like everyone else, they do what they're told. You can't blame them for losing your men.

You write how your corpsman repeatedly exposed himself to hostile fire to tend injured Marines. You write how he was hit in the arm, but continued to aid the wounded. The pencil stub keeps slipping. It is too small. You wish you could write how proud you were of the corpsman — of how far he had come since he first joined your outfit. He used to fall out on every march and he was always late to formation and sloppy. You wish you could convey how very much he hated being posted to the Marines. He joined the Navy, he'd told you, to go to sea, not to run around the rice paddies looking after a lot of neurotic jarheads. You wish you could write how proud he'd become of the Marine insignia your troops had given him and how he'd gotten into a fight with another corpsman who had made fun of the insignia. You want to tell how very bad the fire was when he crawled out to help a wounded squad leader and how he dragged the man back, but the Marine was dead when they reached safety. You ought to be able to put that in reports. You ought to be able to tell your superiors what it was truly like so they wouldn't knock the corpsman's Silver Star down to a Bronze Star or a Commendation Medal. But there is no place for that on reports.

You think of Gunny Mac. He'd been your platoon sergeant for a few weeks over a year ago — when you were on Okinawa with India Company. He was doing his job when he was killed. You had ordered him to have his platoon assault some enemy machine-gun positions. You knew it would be bad — that you'd lose men. But you knew you had to get the enemy machine guns or you'd all be in trouble. Gunny Mac had been the first one to cross the trench line, and an enemy .50 struck him on the jaw and tore off the back of his skull. The book would say that he didn't rate a medal — that he was just doing his job — but the book couldn't know what it took to lead that charge.

There are others — many others — who rate medals and recognition. You want to write them all up, but you know you can't. You know Battalion would never approve them — that every CO feels the same way about his men — that you have to pick the very best and reward them.

You finish writing and put on your boots. You walk to your company office and talk with your first sergeant about the weather and when the monsoons will come and if you can get extra foul-weather gear for the troops. You give your reports and medal requests to the clerks to type.

As you leave the company office you see your corpsman sitting on an empty water can by the side of the tent. His face is in his hands and his body heaves irregularly. You realize he is crying — not loudly, but soft and wet. You touch his shoulder and shake him gently, but he doesn't stop crying and he doesn't say anything.

You get the doctor, and he takes the corpsman to his tent. You wait at your company office to find out what is wrong. Your first sergeant offers you coffee in a tin cup and tells you he had seen many cases like this in World War II, but not many in Vietnam.

The coffee is cold and weak, but you drink it because there isn't anything else to do as you wait. In a little while the doctor comes in and tells you he has sent the corpsman to the hospital ship off Da Nang for a rest. He calls it combat fatigue and says that the corpsman's best friend, a Marine in another company, had been killed yesterday. The corpsman had just learned of it. Coming as it did after your operation was too much for him. The doctor says the corpsman will probably be back from the hospital ship in a week or so.

As you walk toward your tent you see the battalion adjutant and you stop to talk with him. You tell him about the corpsman and ask him if he can hurry the medal request through to Division. He nods and tells you he'll do what he can. You think it would be nice to have the medal waiting when your corpsman returns.

12
The Letter

One of your company clerks stops by your tent and hands you two damp and very limp letters. You read the return addresses and see that one is from a girl you know back home. She was always young and fresh and vibrant. You liked to be with her because she could make you feel that way too. You wonder if she still could. You put her letter aside and open the one from your father.

The rain drums hard on the roof of your tent. The monsoons have begun. It has rained steadily for ten days. There is a sudden splash on the end of the footlocker you are sitting on. A leak. You move to your cot to read the letters.

You lie on your back on the cot and stare at the gray sheets of water falling outside. The rain is coming straight down and you have rolled up the sides of the tent to get as much air as you can. You feel the long ridges of the rubber air mattress pressing into your back. You think of lying on the beach with Peggy. You remember the taste of the salt-water in your mouth and how cold the wind felt until you dried off. You remember talking with Peggy about the future and what you would do. You remember how soft the touch of her hand was and how her hair used to get in the way when you kissed. She would brush it aside and smile at you and laugh softly. And how blue her eyes were.

You turn on your side and begin to read. Your father has gotten a promotion and is thinking of buying a new house. The weather in Connecticut has been very cold and he has built a fire in the fireplace every night for the past week. The dog and the cat are fine. Your stepmother sends her regards.

You hear a curse through the drumbeat of the rain and you look up and see a Marine struggling through the mud. He stumbles and catches himself on a branch. The mud sucks at his boots and he moves very slowly toward your perimeter defenses. One of your sergeants is making his rounds. His squad is on the line and he always takes a pack full of extra rations to them when he checks positions. You can see the bulge the pack makes on his back underneath the poncho. The pack makes him look like a humpback as he fights his way through the mud toward his men.

You open Peggy's letter and hold it to your nose. It still smells very faintly of her. You wonder why girls always perfume their letters. You take a deep breath and decide you don't care why. You like it.

She is still working in New York and writes wonderful long letters telling you how she is decorating her apartment and how you would like the new painting a friend gave her. She writes of the times you had together and how awful the war must be for you. She tells you she bought a book of Robert Frost's poetry for you and is sending it directly.

You laugh to yourself as you remember an autumn day at college when you tried to explain poetry's New Criticism to her. You were building a carefully organized argument about the need for New Criticism in modern poetry when she reached out and touched your hand. You forgot about New Criticism as you held her tightly.

You put the letter down and stare into the wet grayness. You want to hold her again very badly.

A drop of water splashes on your chest and you sit up suddenly — startled. Another leak. You get up and kick your footlocker, but the leak doesn't stop. You open the locker and look for a tent-patching kit you have in there someplace.

The locker smells moldy and everything is damp to the touch. You can't find the kit, so you move your cot away from the leak and begin to read again.

Two sharp rifle shots cut the wetness and you feel your skin tingle in anticipation. You grab your pistol belt and sling it over your shoulder and begin to run toward the perimeter — where the shots came from.

The pounding rain soaks you in a few seconds. The mud grabs at your boots and tries to hold you back. You are only aware of the mud. You hear more shots and a machine gun opens up ahead of you. From the sound it makes you can tell it's one of yours.

As you reach your lines you see a Marine walking toward you very slowly. His face is twisted and he looks like he has been crying, but it's too wet to tell. You recognize him as one of the sergeant's men and you slow to ask him about the shots.

He holds up an empty haversack and you can see two bullet holes — about ten inches apart — cut neatly through the pack.

"Dead," is all he says.

You see two Marines carrying the sergeant's body back toward the CP. Another Marine is dragging the body of the enemy sniper who killed his squad leader.

The rain feels very cold. You look down as the men carry the body past you. You realize you have been holding Peggy's letter in your left hand the whole time. The ink is hopelessly blurred. You crumple it into a ball and drop it into the mud and begin to walk back to your tent to make your report.

13
The Souvenir

Four hearts. You close the bidding and lean back on your cot to study the dummy. The contract will give you a rubber. You can make an extra trick if your finesse for the queen of diamonds works.

You have been playing bridge since breakfast and soon it will be too hot to continue. The air is very still and the mosquito netting hangs limply where the sides of the tent have been rolled up. The rains will be coming again soon — you can smell them. But it's still hot.

You decide Jack has the queen and you finesse through him. It works. You announce the rest of the hand is a laydown. You are just beginning to tally up the score when a runner from the battalion headquarters tells you that you are all wanted at the CP right away.

You have been through many alerts — so many you can't remember them all. But you never know. The battalion commander looks grim. He tells you that two battalions of ARVN rangers on a sweep have run into trouble south of Da Nang, that Marine battalions from all the enclaves are being lifted in, that you have to be ready to go in an hour. He tells you that you will be heli-lifted to a point near Que Son where you will link up with two other battalions.

You walk quickly to your company office and issue instructions to your staff. They must be ready in forty-five minutes. They can draw extra ammunition and rations from battalion supply.

You don't know how long you'll be in the field. You take two tins of spiced beef and a can of apricots from your C rations and roll them in your poncho with an extra pair of socks. You tie the poncho to the back of your pistol belt. You don't like packs — even though you can carry more. Packs slow you down. You make sure your magazines are loaded and you wipe them with an oily rag. Your gunnery sergeant comes by and gives you a map of the area you are to be in.

You put on your pistol belt. You don't buckle it — you let it hang by its shoulder straps. As you walk toward Jack's tent you wonder what this operation will be like. You've been on eight combat operations and several patrols. You never get used to them.

Jack is loading his magazines and you sit on his cot and take a cigar from your pocket and light it.

"Just a little one," Jack says, "just a little nick in the leg. Just enough to get sent home."

You laugh. "I'd rather get it in the arm."

"They never send you home with one of those."

"You've got a point," you say.

He pulls on his pack and hangs his helmet on one of his canteens.

"You got another cigar?"

You hand him one and stand up. It's like before a football game or a wrestling match. The butterflies are churning in your stomach and you can't make them stop. Maybe it's the air. Maybe it's those ARVN rangers. Maybe you've been in Vietnam too long.

The helicopters are warming up. You turn your back to them as you wait with your heli-team. The wind from the rotors kicks up dust and you can feel pebbles stinging your back. The motor's noise is deep and resonant and your whole body vibrates to its rhythm.

You are all the way aft — near the tail of the helicopter. There are no benches and you sit on the deck with your knees under your chin. You can see out the port hatch and the interior smells of oil and exhaust fumes.

You pass over Que Son and you look for the area you're to land in. You search the terrain for friendly troops — something to orient you when you land. But you don't land. They are taking you toward a large horseshoe-shaped hill about a mile from the village. You see tracers flashing by the helicopter and splashes in the rice paddies where rounds are hitting. You squeeze your legs a little closer to your body and you rub your hand against your holster.

The helicopter begins its descent. The pilot is

autorotating to avoid the slower circular approach. There is a loud crack above the roar of the engine. An oil line ruptures and a black smear begins to grow on the deck near you. You realize you are taking rounds. You want to run — to move — to get out of the helicopter.

The helicopter touches the paddy and the crew chief is waving to your heli-team to exit. You push the man ahead of you — to hurry him. There is a sharp crack and you feel a burning shock in your leg. You think an electrical circuit must have been knocked loose — that it brushed against your leg. But you're sitting down and you see blood coming through your trouser.

Suddenly, there are several sharp explosions and the interior of the aircraft is alive with hot metal. You throw yourself flat and cover your face with your right arm. When you look up the helicopter is rising.

You have been shot through the leg and taken shrapnel in one arm. The machine gunner was shot through the buttocks and the crew chief has metal fragments in his hand. You look at your leg — still not believing it — and you see a .30 caliber bullet lying next to you. You touch it. It's still warm. It went through your leg and hit the machine-gun stanchion.

The crew chief cuts off your boot and rips your trouser leg open. He ties a compress from his first-aid packet around your leg.

The leg doesn't hurt. It's numb. You watch the crew chief as he aids the machine gunner. You begin to realize what has happened. You wiggle your toes and flex your leg slightly. You decide that nothing is broken and you lean back on your elbow.

You're very angry. They tried to kill you. You want to hurt them, but you feel helpless. You see the machine gun swinging in the hatch and you pull yourself to it, chamber a round, and begin firing wildly at the ground. The crew chief pulls you away and you lie back on the deck and smoke the cigarette he gives you.

You look at your leg and you wonder if you'll ever play football again. The leg is beginning to throb now and you roll onto your side to be more comfortable. You feel the bullet in your pocket and you take it out and look at it. It is almost perfect. There is only a slight bulge at the tip where it struck the stanchion.

You untie the compress and carefully remove it. There is an exit hole about the size of a half-dollar and bits of muscle protrude. The muscle is pink and contrasts sharply with the blood. You cover it quickly and retie it.

You wish the helicopter would get you back to the aid station. The leg begins to hurt and you begin to worry.

There are corpsmen waiting as you land — the pilot radioed ahead. Careful hands place you on a stretcher. You protest — you're able to limp to the aid station — you don't want to be carried.

They bring you into the operating room and place the stretcher on two sawhorses. Everyone is asking questions and writing things down and sticking needles into you. You decide you like the attention.

You can see the doctors working on you, but you're dead from the waist down. It's like they're working on someone else and you're watching. It strikes you as very funny and you begin to laugh.

The shots they have given you make you sleepy. You show the doctors the bullet and they smile. You hold the bullet very tightly as they carry you out of the operating room. It's your souvenir. You earned it.

14
The Hospital

It is a week before Christmas and it is snowing
lightly in Japan and seems very cold after the heat
of Vietnam. You pull the wool army blanket up to
your chin as the litter bearers carry you from the
bus to the hospital's admitting center. You feel very
snug and the slight smell of mothballs from the blanket makes you think of taking winter clothes out of
storage at home.

You hand your medical records to a corpsman
and he gives you an identification bracelet with your
name and wounds on it. A clerk tells the litter bearers where your ward is, and they carry you toward
the elevator.

On your way you recognize a corpsman who was
in your company a year before. He doesn't see you
at first, but you shout to him and he comes over
and you talk about old times. He tells you several
men from your first company who had been
wounded have come through the hospital.

A corpsman drops your leg onto the end of the bed as you are transferred from the stretcher to your new home. The pain rises through your body like an electric shock. They give you a morphine shot, and when the drug takes effect you sink back into the silky-smooth world only a hard narcotic can produce. The corpsman says he's sorry, but you don't care.

It is almost three hours before your doctor arrives. No one has examined your wounds or changed your dressings for five days. As the doctor cuts the cast from your leg you know it is going to be bad. You don't want to look at the leg, but you smell it, so you sneak a glance. You catch your breath when you begin to feel nauseous at what you see. The leg is not a part of you, you think. It is only connected to you by pain — you can't move it, you can't control it.

You watch your doctor as he gently feels for the ends of the gauze drains that have been put through the shattered channel the bullet left in your leg. You begin to think it will be easy — that there is no feeling left — until the doctor touches the first drain and tries to pull it out. Explosions of pain race up and down your leg and your body trembles in spite of your efforts to control it. You grasp the end of the bed as hard as you can. There is something playing on the radio — a march — and you fasten your mind on it and try to concentrate on the music to keep the swirling redness from overcoming you.

The doctor is saying something to one of the nurses, but you don't listen. You watch him move away from your bed and you begin to relax. He tells you the wound is clean and looks good, but it is too early to tell yet how soon they will close it. He says he has to put new drains in because the wound must heal from the inside out. He says it will hurt. It does. But you're ready for it this time. When you know what is coming — what to expect — it's easier to take.

When the doctor leaves, you look at the man in the next bed. He was an officer in your battalion and was wounded when you were. You never knew him very well before, but there is a lot of time to get acquainted now.

"Pretty bad?" he asks.

You nod. He hasn't had his dressings changed yet and he looks worried. "That music saved me," you tell him. "I think I would have passed out if it hadn't been for that."

"God, I'm a coward when it comes to pain," he says. "I want a shot before they do that to me. You were great — you didn't scream once." He shudders.

"I didn't have time to scream. It hurt too much anyway."

"Jesus, I almost threw up when he pulled out that drain."

"I'm glad I couldn't see it." You lean back on the bed and begin to feel the tension draining from your body.

You suddenly feel very dirty and realize you haven't washed since you came out of the field. You ask one of the corpsmen for a pan of hot water and some soap and a wash cloth. It's not much of a bath, but the cloth is black with dirt when you finish and you feel a lot better.

The doctor said he would return the next day to look at your wounds. You ask each passing corpsman where the doctor is now and when he usually comes and if he'll change the dressings again. But they don't know. It's suppertime when you see the doctor come into the room and you flatten yourself against the bed and grab the rails, trying to ready yourself.

He smiles and asks you how you feel and says not to worry because he won't look at the wounds for another day. You thank him and enjoy a meal for the first time since you arrived. You decide you're going to be all right and that you can take anything he does to you.

You begin to remember it's Christmas and that they must have sent a telegram to your home informing them of your wounds. You think how worried your father will be. You told them not to send a telegram — that it wasn't serious enough — that you didn't want to upset anyone — but you know they always send telegrams.

The nurse tells you there is a phone in the hall and you decide to try and telephone the States. You have no idea what time it will be there, but that isn't important. The nurse fixes a wheelchair for you with an outstretched board to rest your leg on and you wheel yourself down the hall to the phone. The left wheel sticks and the chair keeps turning, but you finally make it.

Your father received the telegram only minutes before your call. He sounds much worse than you feel and you are very glad you are talking to him. You tell him it isn't a bad wound and you probably won't lose your leg. He tells you to do whatever the doctors say and you know he is better.

The next dressing change isn't so bad. You don't need music this time. You don't grasp the bed so hard.

Some members of the Red Cross and some officers' wives come by during the day and decorate your room with paper Santa Clauses and Christmas trees and red and green bells. It is only two days before Christmas, and one of the nurses gives you a drink of eggnog. Liquor is forbidden in the wards, but Christmas is a time to celebrate. It tastes good and you drink too much of it and have trouble working your wheelchair.

You give some money to a friend who is an outpatient and he buys a bottle of brandy for you. You decide to save the brandy until Christmas Eve and drink it then.

A choir from the dependents' grammar school comes around on Christmas Eve and they sing carols and stare awkwardly at your bandages. You notice how clean and wholesome they look. And how new their clothes are. They wish you a merry Christmas and move down the hall to another room. You can hear them singing through the closed door and it sounds a thousand miles away.

A Negro corpsman dressed in a Santa Claus suit comes by giving out Red Cross Christmas gifts. You get a sock filled with rubber shower sandals, writing materials, and hard candy. You thank him and think about what Christmas in Vietnam must be like. For the first time you realize that someone else commands your men now. Those troops you trained and fought with aren't yours anymore. You miss the responsibility. You think about your men who have been killed and you decide to write to their families. Families are important at Christmas.

You're suddenly very tired. You pour some brandy into the plastic water cup that sits on the stand next to your bed. You don't really want it, but you drink it anyway. You lie back and look out the window. It is a clear night and the stars are very bright. From somewhere down the corridor you hear the muffled sound of "Silent Night." You close your eyes and think of Vietnam again — and you hope the carol is right.

15
The Ear

You report to the sub unit at Camp Courtney, Okinawa, and stand awkwardly before the adjutant's desk while he scans your records. Your leg is bothering you and you'd like to sit down, but you don't ask to.

You decide right away that you don't like the adjutant. It's more than just the normal feeling that an infantry line officer has for everyone else. Maybe it's the adjutant's neatly pressed uniform, or the fact that he will be reassigning you, or the way he wears his single Vietnamese campaign ribbon. He tells you to check in to the Bachelor Officers' Quarters and he'll find something for you to do.

The Officers' Club opens at noon. You and another transient officer are the only ones there. The two of you drink martinis and roll dice from a polished leather cup to see who pays. You are losing, but it doesn't make any difference. Liquor is cheap and you have a lot of back pay to spend.

You have lost your third round and are asking the bartender for two more martinis when you hear your name called. A friend from your days at the Schools Battalion in the States makes his way toward you grinning broadly.

"How the hell are you?" You shake hands. "I heard you were hit — lost your leg."

"No, the leg's just a little bit stiff," you tell him. Rumors are funny. You remember some of your troops coming through the hospital in Japan telling you they'd heard you had been killed. "What are you doing now?" you ask him.

He tells you he's the commanding general's aide-de-camp and offers to buy you a drink. By dinnertime you are both quite drunk and you decide you need some fresh air.

The day has been warm and humid. You sit on the porch in the evening cool and watch lights flickering along the coast winding north to Kin Village and beyond. You feel very much alone. You miss your troops and your old friends and you wonder how they are doing. You know you don't have much chance of landing another infantry command and you begin thinking of what you will do when you're released from the Marine Corps in four months. It's appropriate, you think, that your troop-leading career began and will end on Okinawa.

The next day the adjutant tells you that a lieutenant colonel in charge of transient personnel is looking for an officer to take over the R and R Center for troops from Vietnam. You're to report to him at noon at Camp Butler.

You like the colonel. He tells you what has to be done — what he expects — but he leaves the details to you. The R and R Center will be located at Camp Hauge and will be the only billet there. You like that too.

A flight departs Okinawa every other day returning a planeload of personnel to Vietnam. They have had five days of R and R in Okinawa. The plane will pick up a new R and R load in Da Nang and Chu Lai and return in the evening. You brief the troops on what they can do and where they can go; you give them a quick medical check and assign them a rack and a wall locker. Then you turn them loose.

Your admin chief is a gunnery sergeant from a Force Recon unit near Chu Lai. He was wounded there — his fifth Purple Heart in four wars. The gunny has a problem with liquor, but he likes the troops and he always seems to get the job done. You think how you would have never tolerated drinking on duty a short while ago. Vietnam has a way of loosening things up.

You usually go with the gunny to greet the new arrivals at the air station. There isn't much to do and you like to see if you know any of the incoming R and R personnel.

Most of the troops are so anxious to get out on liberty that they don't take the time to eat or lock up their valuables before they go. Every flight has its share of men getting drunk and being rolled on their first night of liberty. With no money, there isn't much to do but send them back to Vietnam on an early flight.

You arrange for box lunches to be placed on the buses. You know the men won't take the time to eat once they're given liberty. But they might eat the lunches on the bus and that might help them stay sober a little longer.

You have been on Okinawa for about a month. It's a Thursday evening and a light rain is falling. The flight from Vietnam is late. You and the gunny are sitting in the flight terminal drinking coffee and watching the rain bead on the windows. When the corporal at the desk tells you that the plane is landing, you put on your cap and raincoat and walk across the runway to meet the aircraft.

The troops stumble out of the belly of the transport plane. They don't know where they're going, but they only have five days and they're in a hurry. You watch the gunny directing them to the buses when you hear your name called softly behind you.

You turn around and find a young Negro sergeant facing you. He's one of your old squad leaders. He salutes and you shake hands and walk with him toward the buses. The headlights cut sharp paths through the rain and within the beams the water seems to be exploding in all directions.

You are happy to see the sergeant. You talk over old times, and he hands you a small package and tells you it's from a staff sergeant in your old company. You ask him what it is, but he just smiles.

You wait until you have briefed the troops and released them before you go into your office and open the package. There is a note stuck in a corner of the package and you read it before you untie the box. It says simply: "This one's for you, Lieutenant. From the old India Company."

India Company was your first company in the Marine Corps. Some of the men from that company are in Vietnam now. You know what's in the box even before you open it. You used to joke with some of the NCO's in India Company about how the Turks accounted for enemy dead in Korea — by cutting off ears. You remember a staff sergeant visiting you in the field hospital before you were evacuated to Japan. He had said he'd get you an ear.

You open the package. Carefully wrapped in waxed paper is a small and very shriveled ear. The blood on it has dried to a brown stain.

You rewrap the ear in waxed paper and retie the packet.

You don't feel horrified at the ear on your desk. You feel very humble. You feel very proud. It is a tribute to you. If you were a girl you'd cry.

The gunny comes in and sees you sitting there, staring at the package.

"Everything all right?" he asks.

You hand him the package and the note.

He opens the package and reads the note. He looks at you and nods very slowly. "That's very nice, sir." He understands.

You go back to your quarters and pour yourself a brandy. You think of the old days — with India Company. And you think of Vietnam. But it all seems so far away. You're due to be rotated to the States and released soon. There will be no more India Companies, no more Vietnams for you. You realize that a part of your life has gone and that it can never return. You open your desk and take out some graduate school brochures. You are looking at universities in several different areas of the country. You think you might like Los Angeles.

16
The Homecoming

From thirty thousand feet the Pacific looks like an unending sheet of corrugated metal. The waves are the bulges. You can't see them move at all. But you don't care; you're going home.

You don't feel excited. You don't want to kiss the ground when the plane lands at Travis Air Force Base near San Francisco. You thought it would be different — like it was the first time you returned from Okinawa. You were excited about coming home then. You felt like kissing the ground, although you didn't. You felt like telling everyone you met that you had just returned from fourteen months in places like Japan and Okinawa and the Philippines. You wanted to tell them about the things you'd seen and done. You wanted to hear what was happening in the country you hadn't seen for over a year. You were proud and happy. You were glad to be home, but you missed the Orient. It's different this time. You're just tired.

The check-in procedure is routine and dull. A couple of bored clerks stamp your orders and you stand in line and wait to hear a major tell you to report to Treasure Island for mustering out. He says it will take them about a week to give you various medical exams and process your records. He doesn't seem interested and you can't decide whether he doesn't care about any transient or whether you have been singled out because you're leaving the service in a few days. He says a bus will be leaving for TI in about an hour, and you had better make it because it's the only bus today.

The ride from Travis to Treasure Island takes several hours. You are sitting next to a Marine sergeant who has just returned from Vietnam. You catch him looking at your medals and you smile and offer him a cigarette. He takes it and thanks you and asks which unit you were with. You tell him and he asks about some friends of his who had been transferred to your outfit, but after you were wounded. You tell him you have just come back from three months in the hospital in Japan and that you haven't been in Vietnam for about five months.

The sergeant had been stationed at Chu Lai and he was in Vietnam for a full tour — thirteen months. He's glad to be home. He tells you about his family and asks what you are going to do. You tell him you are leaving the Marine Corps and going to graduate school at UCLA. He says he doesn't blame you and he wishes he could go back to school, but he's got a dozen years in the Corps and he has a wife and three children to worry about.

You talk about how different the States look and how fast the cars seem to move. You talk about the weather and how cool it is. You talk about the sergeant's next duty station — Quantico, Virginia. You don't talk about Vietnam. Neither of you wants to. Neither of you has to.

The BOQ at Treasure Island is full. They are hosting a conference of supply officers and there is no room for you. The Filipino steward tells you you should have made reservations — that there is nothing they can do now. You'll have to check into the Marine's Memorial Club in downtown San Francisco. They will give you a special per diem allowance to pay the bills. They have a room at the BOQ for tonight, but you'll have to share it with two other Marines. And you'll have to check out in the morning.

You're too tired to argue about it or to worry. You carry your suitcase to the room they assigned you and you collapse on one of the beds. You don't bother to undress and the next thing you know it's three hours later and there are voices in the room. You sit up and you feel your skin tingling as you search for your pistol and you can't find it under your bed where you always used to keep it. Suddenly, you remember you don't need the pistol anymore and you lean back and stare at the voices.

"Sorry, sir, we didn't mean to wake you." The speaker is a very junior second lieutenant. He and another lieutenant are standing by the door and seem worried about having disturbed you.

"Relax, Lieutenant," you tell him. You introduce

yourself and tell them you've just gotten back from overseas and you're getting out of the Marines in a week and all you want to do is sleep. But you're not tired anymore.

"You were in Vietnam, sir?" one of the lieutenants asks.

You nod. You know they want to hear some of your experiences, but you don't feel like telling them sea stories. It won't make any difference; they'll have to learn things the hard way. You suggest that you all go down to the bar for a drink. You button your uniform coat and you smile to yourself as the lieutenants sneak a glance at your rows of ribbons. Junior officers, you think, are all medal-crazy. You were. But you aren't that way anymore. You know what medals mean.

You order a gin-and-tonic and you watch as the bartender squeezes a lime onto the ice. The ice steams and crackles and the drink is very good. You couldn't get limes on Okinawa and you had forgotten how much better a gin-and-tonic is with limes. You down the drink in two gulps and ask for another.

"Who were you with, sir?" one of the lieutenants asks.

You haven't been a captain very long and the sir bothers you. You tell the lieutenants to call you by your first name, that you won't put them on report.

They both grin. They have just graduated from Officers' Basic School at Quantico. They are en route to Vietnam for their first assignment. You don't envy them. At least you had eighteen months of the infantry before you went into combat. You finish your second drink.

You tell them who you were with and what they can expect. You tell them that you can't say how it will be for them because it is different for everybody. You tell them to remember their training because it is good and because they'll need it. You tell them about booby traps and where the VC like to place them. You explain what they should do when they get their first assignments — probably as platoon leaders. They want to know about snakes. You resist the temptation to tell them there are cobras and vipers everywhere. You laugh and say that everybody worries about snakes, but you never saw more than two the whole time you were there. You tell them about the heat and the dysentery and you tell them not to worry about either because there's nothing they can do about them.

As the gin begins to take hold you feel less and less like talking. You remind them to look after their men and that if they do they'll be all right. You tell them the most valuable thing they can take to Vietnam is a good sense of humor. You finish your third drink and tell them you have to go out to dinner with a friend. You lie because you want to be alone.

They are different than you are — they haven't been to Vietnam yet. They haven't seen combat. You know their questions are sincere, that you felt the same way only a year before, but you don't want to answer them. You belong to different worlds.

You change into civilian clothes and walk across

the base toward the bus stop. The sun is beginning to go down and there are sailboats completing a race on the bay. You look toward San Francisco and watch the boats until the bus comes. You take a seat in the very back. You still don't like people behind you.

You walk to Union Square and stand near the St. Francis Hotel and watch the people and cars moving past. You are amazed at how well dressed the people are and at how shiny the cars are. The streets are clean and the square is very green. You watch a group of people gathering near one corner of the square. Some of them are carrying placards, but most are simply standing there. You can make out the lettering on one placard. It says: "Get out of Vietnam."

You cross the street and move into the outer reaches of the crowd. The people don't seem to be as well dressed as most of the passersby, and you feel out of place in a clean shirt and coat and tie.

There were many reports overseas about the peace movement back home. Most of the men didn't think much about it. You were usually too busy or too tired. When it was discussed, the peace movement was usually the subject of a certain amount of derision. And it was usually dismissed as being conducted by people who were ignorant about what was happening.

A bearded orator — about your age — regales the passersby with tales of napalmed villages and maimed children. Some of the crowd nods in agreement. The orator builds to a fever pitch and his arms flail and his body shakes with righteous indignation as he tells the people of San Francisco the war is immoral, illegal, and unjust.

A girl stands near you. She is pretty with long hair hanging to the small of her back. She is holding some posters and seems to be dressed better than the others. You ask her who the speaker is. She tells you he is from UC, Berkeley, and that he is a member of the Students for a Democratic Society. You ask her about the maiming and napalming and she hands you a printed circular with some grisly photographs of flaming houses and burned children. You ask her if the orator has ever seen any flaming houses and burned children. She recoils slightly and cocks her head to one side and stares at you before she says he is only a sophomore at Berkeley.

You walk across the square and down the hill to Powell Street to get a cable car. You ride the car to the outskirts of Chinatown and stroll slowly along streets crowded with oriental shops and restaurants until you get to Grant Avenue. People are everywhere and everyone seems to be rushing. You stop at a small restaurant and have a martini. You decide you aren't hungry and you finish the drink and leave.

You catch a cab back to the bus station and wait a few minutes before the Treasure Island bus arrives. A couple of drunken sailors are waiting too and they are telling each other the best way to sneak off the base. The discussion ends when one of the sailors gets sick.

The two lieutenants are gone when you get to

your room. You're glad. You decide on a nightcap before you go to bed and you walk slowly through the lounge to the bar. There is a large bulletin board on the wall next to the bar, and you remember the peace rally as you pass it. You take out the circular with the photos of burned children and tack it on the board next to an announcement of the supply officers' conference.

You smile at the circular and laugh and go into the bar, thinking how much better limes make a gin-and-tonic taste.

17
The Promise

Some promises can be broken. You know when they're made they will never be kept and as long as you know it, it doesn't matter so much when you don't keep them. The hard ones are those you don't make out loud — the ones you make to yourself. You can delay these promises; you can tell yourself that they don't count because no one else knows; you can even pretend you never made them. But in the end you have to keep them. You do it because you know if you don't they will keep coming back in various ways and reminding you they are unfulfilled. And you fulfill them because you have to and you want to and that's why you made them in the first place. Most of them are unpleasant. And the most unpleasant of all is the promise you made yourself to visit Gunny Mac's widow when you returned to California.

You are scheduled to catch a flight to New York later in the day. It will be your first time to see your family and friends on the East Coast since you went to Vietnam over a year before. You like to travel by airplane. Even though you have flown dozens of times, you still get a thrill when you realize the plane's wheels have left the runway and you are airborne. There is an excitement too about an airport. You like the bustle and activity — travelers departing and waiting and arriving, farewells and greetings — even if you have a long wait for a plane. But today in your car on the way to Gunny Mac's widow you don't think about the airport, or your flight, or your family and friends. Today you think about the Gunny and Vietnam. And you think about what you have to do.

It's easy to find the house. It's a small, brick ranch house standing on a corner. The grass needs mowing and the front gate swings loosely on its hinges — moving slightly as the breeze directs. You know it is the place the first time you drive by because you can read the name on the mailbox. But you tell yourself that you have to check — you have to make sure. So you drive by again.

You pull the car up to the curb about a hundred meters from the driveway and sit there, trying to think about what you will say. You want to rehearse it so you won't say anything to upset his family.

You take a pad and pencil from the seat next to you and begin to write down what you think you ought to say. Nothing seems right and in a few minutes the paper is filled with scratched-out phrases and half-finished sentences. You put the pad down and light a cigarette and stare at the house.

You begin to think about the day the Gunny was killed and you try to force it out of your mind. You remember how hot it was and how thirsty you were and what a bad time you were having from the enemy. The Gunny knew it too and he knew that the Viet Cong machine guns had to be knocked out. You remember how loud the firing sounded and how everything became so very still for you when you saw the bullet hit the Gunny's face. The firing hadn't stopped, of course, as you thought for a moment then. At least the firing hadn't stopped for you.

You are suddenly very thirsty and you decide to get something to drink before you pay your respects. You see a coffee shop down the street and you start the car and drive to it.

You order a cup of coffee and sit at the counter, still trying to find the right words. You are the only customer and the waiter keeps talking to you, but you don't really listen to him. You hear just enough to nod at the right time and mumble an occasional yes or no. Your thoughts are elsewhere — until the man asks if you heard what happened to the Marine's widow down the street.

You tell him that you haven't and he shakes his head and leans forward on the counter as if he were going to whisper a confidence to you. You smell the coffee in your cup and the weaker smell of stale grease and day-old pastries in the display case along the counter. You look very hard at a smudged fingerprint on the glass in front of you, but your ears are carefully tuned to the man and what he is saying.

"Poor woman," he says very slowly. "Guess she was so upset by her husband getting killed and all that she didn't know what she was doing." He shakes his head again.

"What did she do?"

" 'Course, I probably would have wanted to know too. Can't say as I blame her for it. Still, it must have been bad for the kids."

"I still didn't catch what it was she did."

"Gettin' a closed casket and all. I guess she wanted to make sure. They say her husband had been in a lot of wars — he was a Marine, you know — and they're always making mistakes. Must have been rough, though."

You feel a chill of excitement and you shiver. You know what the bullet did to the Gunny's head. You know you couldn't have identified him if you hadn't seen him hit.

"She opened the casket?" you ask — not wanting to hear the answer.

"She sure did. Right there at the wake with the kids and all looking on. I guess it got so bad for her that she just had to know. Must have been bad, though."

You knock on the door and when the Gunny's widow answers you introduce yourself. She asks you in. You tell her that you can only stay for a few minutes — that you have to catch a plane. You stare at the drapes as you talk with her. They are very dusty. Everything you say seems to have no meaning. The words are clichés. But you say them because you have to and she doesn't seem to mind that they have all been said before and probably better said at that. She apologizes that her children aren't there to meet you, and you say that you would have liked to meet them too. She offers you a cup of coffee, but you tell her that you really have to go. She nods and says that she understands.

At the door she thanks you for coming. You ask her if there is anything you can do. She replies that everything has been well taken care of. You tell her again how very sorry you are and suddenly you become disgusted with the words. They seem empty and hollow and only likely to stir up old feelings of the dread and agony of irremediable loss. She seems to know what you are thinking and as you turn to go she tells you that the words don't matter, that your coming would have pleased the Gunny very much, and that he often spoke of you in his letters. She says the Gunny always felt he could turn you into a pretty good Marine if he had more time to train you. You laugh and thank her and walk through the gate to your car parked down the street. You hurry because you feel your eyes growing wet and you don't want anyone to see.

You're glad that it's done. But you're glad that you came. It was one of those promises you had to keep. In the car on the way to the airport you begin to think about your flight home.

18
The Parade

The small white sentry post that guards the main gate at Camp Pendleton squats in the middle of the road. Cars approaching it from either direction must stop there unless they have a base sticker. You have never been to the base as a civilian and from force of habit you almost drive through without stopping. But you are a civilian now and you stop your car and ask the sentry for a guest pass. You half expect a salute and when it doesn't come you feel a twinge of disappointment. The sentry gives you a pass and waves you through.

It is spring in California and it has been drizzling for several days. The rain has turned the foliage a bright green and you think how pretty it is now and how brown and burnt and ugly it will become when the summer sun has baked the base for a few weeks.

Ahead of you on the road you can see two columns of men — one on each side of the road — and you slow your car as you approach them. They are an infantry battalion and they're strung out along the road for half a mile. The men look quite tired and the officers and staff are running up and down the columns shouting encouragement and prodding the slow and the lazy.

"Close it up, Spencer. I want you people asshole to belly button when we go home."

"Close it up, damn it! You look like doggies."

"Goin' home, men. Get them packs squared away. Look like Marines!"

You smile in spite of yourself and you're glad you are riding. You had your days of walking. You look hard at the men as you pass through their ranks to see if you recognize any of them. Their equipment looks brand-new, and you guess they have just received a fresh issue and are getting ready to go overseas. You don't recognize any of them and you begin to speed up as you clear their ranks. You watch the men fade in your rearview mirror and become smaller. Soon their uniforms and packs and cartridge belts match the green foliage by the side of the road, and you can only tell there are men there by the movements. You look up at a sign indicating the start of Basilone Road and when you check the mirror again you can't see the men anymore.

You turn onto Basilone Road. It was named for Machine Gun John Basilone — a Marine hero in World War II. You wonder what it was like fighting in the islands in the South Pacific and you wonder if it was much different from Vietnam. You slow the car down as you pass Camp Santa Margarita.

You got a ticket here once for speeding and you instinctively check your speedometer. You decide that you're well within the speed limit and you begin to pick up speed again. It isn't raining now and although the sun hasn't forced its way through the overcast there is a sharp glare on the road. You take a pair of sunglasses from the glove compartment. They are dirty and you hold the wheel with one hand and wipe them on your sleeve before you put them on.

As you enter the area where the Marine Corps trains the graduates of its boot camps in the ways of modern combat, you think back to a regimental problem you had here. And you think about how pleased you were when some of your men — led by Gunny Mac — captured the aggressors' commanding officer.

It is still lunchtime at the ITR (Infantry Training Regiment). You have a few minutes before your appointment at Camp San Mateo and you stop the car near the mess hall and watch the drill sergeants marching their men to and from chow. The singsong cadences and rhythmic commands are old to your ears and you recognize them all. But you know how strange they must seem to these young Marines. You watch and laugh to yourself as one Marine after another gets out of step or makes a wrong turn. They too will learn, you think.

You get out of the car and walk across the parade deck to where a sergeant is holding a class on the hand grenade. He is a tall, well-built young Negro and at first you think you recognize him, but you don't and you lean against a tree and listen.

"This grenade," he points to it, "has a burst radius of twenty meters. When you people throw it, you had better throw it far enough so you don't kill yourself or anybody else. The Marine Corps doesn't have money enough to keep building monuments to unknown soldiers and if you don't wing this thing far enough, that's just what you're going to be." He strips the protective tape from the body of the grenade. "To throw it all you got to do is pull the pin, let the handle fly off, count to three, and let it go." He pulls out the safety pin and lets the spoon fly free. It sails over the front row of troops with a metallic whine. The sergeant counts to three and then tosses the grenade into the stunned Marines. There is a brief scramble as the front row tries to get out of the way. The grenade explodes with a sharp crack and belches a thick cloud of black smoke. Those men in the back, who hadn't moved, begin to laugh. The others do too when they realize that it was only a practice grenade.

The instructor retrieves the still-smoking shell and looks at the troops.

"This was only a joke — for practice. The ones you're going to throw this afternoon are real. And you better not forget it."

He continues his lecture, explaining how the grenade works and why you have to let the spoon fly free. You hear his voice grow weaker as you walk back to your car. It is about five miles to Camp San Mateo and you don't want to be late.

They don't give everyone a parade when he retires. If you have served for thirty years you can have one, but there aren't many thirty-year men around anymore. Thirty years is a long time and thirty years cover a lot of wars. War is the Marine Corps' business and to succeed in the business for that long you need many things — courage, skill, training, a sense of humor. And luck. Your old company's first sergeant has succeeded and this afternoon on the parade deck at Camp San Mateo — with the division CO there and the division band playing — he will retire. He will have a parade.

He will wear his dress blue uniform and he will stand alone in the reviewing stand and take the salute of the rifle companies as they pass in review. He will look good in his uniform because it is a proud uniform and "the Top" is a proud man. The medals on his chest represent three wars and some of those smaller actions that attract no press notices and only seem to be measured in the grief of people back home. He will look good because he represents all the men he has known and fought with over those years. And he will look good to you because he is your friend.

You arrive early. You don't want to see "the Top" before the parade. It's his day and you can see him afterward.

You find a parking space and walk over to your old company office. Your outfit has long since departed, and there is a new unit designation nailed to the door. You open the door and look inside. A clerk looks up from his typing and asks if there is anything he can do for you. You shake your head and tell him that this was your old office and that you are back to watch a parade honoring your first sergeant at his retirement. The clerk laughs and says that the first sergeant stopped by just a few minutes before.

You were to meet another officer who knew "the Top" and who had been overseas with you, but there is no sign of him yet. You walk out to the parade deck and watch the band getting their instruments ready and warming up. You have never cared very much for parades. You used to have a formal guard mount with a drum and bugle team every Friday at the NCO Leadership School. You guess you have seen too many and that they no longer have any meaning.

You hear a shout from across the parade deck and when you look up you see the officer you were to meet and another friend from overseas walking toward you.

"Jesus Christ! It's a regular old home week."

"Yeah, we even got Jack to come down from Laguna Beach."

"What's the matter, no surf today?"

"Couldn't miss this one."

You all shake hands and begin to walk slowly toward the edge of the bleachers. You talk about old times and you're really glad to see them again and especially for them to be at "the Top's" parade.

You discuss — for the tenth time — who was the prettiest girl in the Philippines when you hear the adjutant sounding off to start the parade. You are still across the field from the bleachers and you can't run across now that the parade has begun. You walk quickly over to the row of company offices and sit on the ground near a large bulletin board.

The format of this parade is the same as all the other parades you have seen. Of course, it's special because it's "the Top's." You wonder how much of the thirty years he can remember — what is important to him. You think of your three years in the Marine Corps and you can only imagine what is going through his mind.

When the adjutant calls "Pass in review," and "the Top" takes the reviewing stand, you stand up and you notice that your friends have too. The band is playing some Sousa march and when it passes the stand it breaks into the "Marine's Hymn." The music, you suppose, sums up the thirty years about as well as anything can. When the band finishes the "Marine's Hymn" it begins to play something you know you've heard before, but you can't identify it. Suddenly, you realize it is playing a martial version of "Auld Lang Syne."

You greet "the Top" after the parade, but everyone is pumping his hand and congratulating him and passing around a bottle. You feel out of place — as if you didn't know him anymore and as if you didn't belong here — and you leave quickly and go back to your car.

The trip back to Los Angeles seems long. It is misting slightly now, not hard enough to really clean the windshield but hard enough to require the wipers to be turned on. You want to think about your time in the Marines as you know "the Top" must have thought. You want to remember the pride of pinning on your first lieutenant's bars and the excitement of going overseas and the thrill and agony and sorrow of Vietnam. The song — "Auld Lang Syne" — comes back to you, and you try to remember the places you saw and the things you did and the people you knew. Mostly you try to remember the people. You try to hum the song, but the noise the wipers make doesn't keep time and you can't. Time enough for memories later, you think, and you switch on the car radio as you drive back home.

Other books you will enjoy,
about real kids like you!

☐	42365-7	**Blind Date** R.L. Stine	$2.50
☐	41248-5	**Double Trouble** Barthe DeClements and Christopher Greimes	$2.75
☐	41432-1	**Just a Summer Romance** Ann M. Martin	$2.50
☐	40935-2	**Last Dance** Caroline B. Cooney	$2.50
☐	41549-2	**The Lifeguard** Richie Tankersley Cusick	$2.50
☐	33829-3	**Life Without Friends** Ellen Emerson White	$2.75
☐	40548-9	**A Royal Pain** Ellen Conford	$2.50
☐	41823-8	**Simon Pure** Julian F. Thompson	$2.75
☐	40927-1	**Slumber Party** Christopher Pike	$2.50
☐	41186-1	**Son of Interflux** Gordon Korman	$2.50
☐	41513-7	**The Tricksters** Margaret Mahy	$2.95
☐	41546-8	**Yearbook II: Best All-Around Couple** Melissa Davis	$2.50

PREFIX CODE
0-590-

Available wherever you buy books...
or use the coupon below.

Scholastic Inc.
P.O. Box 7502, 2932 East McCarty Street, Jefferson City, MO 65102

Please send me the books I have checked above. I am enclosing $_____$ (please add $1.00 to cover shipping and handling). Send check or money order– no cash or C.O.D.'s please.

Name_____

Address_____

City_____State/Zip_____

Please allow four to six weeks for delivery. Offer good in U.S.A. only. Sorry, mail order not available to residents of Canada. Prices subject to change.

PNT888

point

THRILLERS

It's a roller coaster of mystery, suspense, and excitement with **thrillers** from Scholastic's Point! Gripping tales that will keep you turning from page to page–strange happenings, unsolved mysteries, and things unimaginable!

Get ready for the ride of your life!

☐	MC40927-1	**Slumber Party** Christopher Pike	**$2.50**
☐	MC40753-8	**Weekend** Christopher Pike	**$2.50**
☐	MC40832-1	**Twisted** R. L. Stine	**$2.50**
☐	MC42365-7	**Blind Date** R. L. Stine	**$2.50**
☐	MC41549-2	**The Lifeguard** Richie Tankersley Cusick	**$2.50**
☐	MC41929-3	**Prom Dress** Lael Littke	**$2.75**
☐	MC42439-4	**Party Line** A. Bates	**$2.75**
☐	MC41858-0	**The Baby-sitter** R. L. Stine	**$2.75**

PREFIX CODE 0-590-

Watch for new titles coming soon!
Available wherever you buy books, or use coupon below.